ER
RJH

EDEimo

Please return / renew by date shown.
You can renew it at:
 norfolk.gov.uk
: 0344 800 8006

D0892240

2016

- 5 JAN 20

# CORNISH KILLING

Chrissie Loveday

NORFOLK LIBRARY AND
INFORMATION SERVICE

| SUPPLIER | AUDIOGO |
| INVOICE No. | |
| ORDER DATE | |
| COPY No. | |

**CHIVERS**

> British Library Cataloguing in Publication Data available

This Large Print edition published by AudioGO Ltd, Bath, 2013.
Published by arrangement with the Author

U.K.  Hardcover     ISBN   978 1 4713 3344 6
U.K.  Softcover     ISBN   978 1 4713 3345 3

Copyright © Chrissie Loveday, 2012

All rights reserved

| NORFOLK LIBRARY AND INFORMATION SERVICE | |
| --- | --- |
| SUPPLIER | AudioGO |
| INVOICE No. | |
| ORDER DATE | |
| COPY No. | |

Printed and bound in Great Britain by
TJ International Limited

# CHAPTER 1

When Emma put the phone down, she shook her head. Typical Charlie.

'Come with me to Cornwall on Saturday,' she had burst out. 'It'll be fab. Help you forget your troubles.'

'But I can't just drop everything and go on holiday.'

'Course you can. Just tell them you're going. Or take a sicky.'

'Grow up Charlie,' she'd snapped.

A remote cottage, left to her by some distant relation sounded amazing. She imagined chintz curtains, roses round the door and wonderful sea views, along with the obligatory cream teas. But then, Charlie always exaggerated these things. On the other hand, she'd been having a really bad time recently and she was certainly due some leave, but this Saturday was impossible. Maybe in a week or so she might manage it. Another phone call the next day and Emma was convinced.

'I'll drive down on Saturday and get things sorted. I'm not sure what sort of state it's in. The old lady was in hospital at the end and it's some time since she died. It may need a clean up, but I expect most things will be there. I'll take some supplies in case. The solicitor's arranging to leave the keys with a neighbour.

Exciting isn't it?' Charlie had enthused.

'I guess so. Look, I can get some holiday and come down next week. I'll travel down on Thursday. If I come by train I can get a lift back with you and save myself the long drive.'

'Brill,' Charlie almost shouted. 'Let me know the train time and I'll pick you up in Penzance.'

'I looked it up already. I should be in Penzance by six-thirty.'

'I'll be there. That gives me plenty of time to get everything in order and suss out the best places to eat. Can't wait to see you,' Charlie had said and hung up.

Emma watched the coasts of Devon and then Cornwall pass by the windows as she sat on the train. It had been a long journey and she was looking forward to seeing Charlie again. She took the postcard out of her handbag and looked at the picture of a rocky cove, deserted and picturesque. Exactly what she needed after the turmoil of last few weeks.

Travelling by train was supposed to relax her instead of the hassle of driving. The problem with the train was that it had given her more time to reflect on her life and where she was going next. It was not a good prospect. She looked forward to talking things through with her best friend.

She and Charlie, Charlotte to her parents and only them, had been at school together

2

and still saw each other regularly. The postcard had arrived yesterday, showing her what she might expect of the place and the proper address of the cottage.

*Hi MA How about this for a place? Gull Cottage, Bodilly Cove. Looks fab doesn't it? C U soon. Love Charlie.*

She smiled. *MA* indeed. Her friend had always used the abbreviation for Emma since they were kids, said it saved writing time. She pushed the card back into her shoulder bag.

The train pulled into Penzance station and she gathered up her luggage and scanned the waiting crowds, looking for Charlie. People were greeting each other and leaving and very soon the platform was clear. No Charlie. Emma sat on the wall, looking over the harbour. Ropes clattered against metal masts and there was the salty tang in the air that everyone expects of the seaside. Classic Charlie. Forgotten the time and probably even what day it was. She was never the most reliable time keeper. But it was going to be fun spending time together again.

Emma glanced at her watch and dialled her friend's number. No reply, and she didn't even have voice mail on. Maybe the battery was flat or she was in one of the reception black spots in Cornwall she'd heard about.

Emma went to the booking office to ask if any message had been left but there was nothing.

'Could I leave a message for someone?' she asked.

'Can do if you wants to, love. Can't guarantee nothing though,' the booking clerk said.

'My friend is supposed to meet me but she isn't here yet. I'm starving so I'll go to the café over there.'

'What's your friend look like?'

'Blonde, about my age, tall and slim. But it's OK, I'll come back when I've grabbed something to eat,' Emma repeated.

'OK, Miss.'

Emma crossed the road and went into the café, lugging her travel bag behind her. She bought a roll and some coffee and sat by the window, looking out in case Charlie arrived.

Half an hour later, she went back to the station.

'You'd best get a taxi,' advised the booking clerk. 'Where you going, love?'

'Bodilly Cove. I think it's a bit out of the way.'

'No kidding. It's middle of nowhere. Not even a road down there. You've got some tidy walk when you gets even as close as the track goes. Nobody goes down there. Much too quiet for most people.'

'Sounds wonderful, just what I need. OK then, thanks. My friend must have broken down or something.'

She gave in and got into one of the waiting

4

cars. The taxi driver took her the seven miles or so and left her at the end of a narrow track that led down a path towards the sea.

'You sure this is where you want to be?' he asked.

'I suppose so. There is something at the end of this, isn't there?' she asked doubtfully.

'There's a cottage or two. You're quite certain this was the address your friend gave you?'

'Well, yes. She wrote it on this postcard.'

'Must be right then.'

'Do you have a phone number I can call if I need a taxi again?' she asked, nervous now. The taxi driver gave her a card. At least she wouldn't be totally cut off if she needed help.

'Cheers. Hope you meet up with your friend.'

Dusk was already starting to darken the narrow track and Emma hoped she was going in the right direction. It was narrow with high hedges so she couldn't see very far ahead of her. At last, she caught a glimpse of the sea crashing over rocks far below her. She paused for a brief rest and hauled her bag up onto her shoulder again.

Why on earth had she brought so much stuff? Charlie had said she should pack waterproofs and walking boots or shoes, as they planned some hikes along the coastal footpath. Maybe she should stop and change into the boots right now to save carrying them.

There was a rustling in the hedgerow beside her and she jumped, her heart beating ridiculously fast. A fox darted across her path and she laughed at her stupid fears. The animal paused, unafraid and with eyes shining almost green in the fading light, then it ran away.

Emma shook her head. This counted as the countryside after all and foxes were everywhere these days. She felt jumpy and not a little worried. Where on earth was this damned cottage and what would she do if Charlie didn't come back to let her in? Presumably, her car would have been left in the space at the top of the track, if this really was the only way down? She hadn't seen the little yellow peril, as it was known.

After what felt like miles of trudging along the rough path, she saw a rooftop through the hedge. With a sigh of weariness she pushed through the broken down gate. It looked pretty dilapidated and with no sign of lights, seemed rather uninviting. She knocked on the door, without hope. She'd have words to say to Charlie when she finally turned up. She tried the handle and the door opened.

'Hello? Charlie?' she called. 'Anyone?'

It remained silent and quite dark. Had she come to the right place? She looked for the light switch and but couldn't find it. She had a little torch in her bag and she shone it round. The place looked grubby and unlived in. She gave a shiver and dumping her bag she pushed open nearest the door. It was a pretty basic kitchen. A cooker attached to a large calor gas bottle, a sink and a large kitchen table. There was a box of candles and some matches sitting on the draining board. That seemed ominous. She lit several candles and felt slightly comforted by having a little light.

'There doesn't even seem to be any electricity,' she muttered to herself. Nor was there any signs at all of someone living there.

She walked round the rooms but it was all impersonal and very empty. No sign that Charlie had even been here. She must have come to the wrong place entirely. She heard a noise outside and went to the door. 'Hello?' she called nervously. 'Is that you Charlie?'

'Hello. Saw the light. What are you doing here?'

'I've was expecting to be staying here.'

'You're not the girl who was s'posed to be coming here?' came a gruff male voice. ''Specting you last weekend we was. Got the place opened up and all.'

'I'm one of the girls. My friend Charlie was supposed to be coming here last Saturday. She's just inherited this place. I was to join her today but she didn't turn up to meet me. I suppose this is Gull Cottage? Bodilly Cove? The taxi driver left me at the top and said it was down here.'

'It is, right enough.'

7

'Do you know where my friend is?'

'Haven't seen nothing of her.' He looked even more shifty than before and wiped his mouth on the back of his sleeve. 'She never turned up so I s'posed she'd changed her mind. Her loss. Didn't know anyone else was s'posed to be coming.'

'I only decided last week. Couldn't get away when she came down so I came today instead. She was supposed to meet me at Penzance. I got a taxi when she didn't arrive at the station.'

'Yip. Charlotte something was s'posed to be coming. Who are you then?'

'Emma. Emma Peterson. And you?'

'Rob Grenville. Owner of the place next door. Well, not exactly next door. Bit of a way along. What you planning to do?'

'I don't know. Stay here tonight at least, I suppose. I need to find out what's happened to Charlie. Is that OK?'

'Suit yourself. Nothing in though and a long way from the shops. Nothing ready here for anyone to stay. Maybe you'd best go back to Penzance and stay in a hotel or summat.'

'It's getting late. I sent the taxi away. Anyhow, I think I'd prefer to wait till tomorrow. I had a roll in town and some coffee. I'll manage for tonight. Isn't there any electricity?'

'Not this far out there ain't. You got gas for the cooker and candles. Not sure if there's any gas left, mind you. Maybe some oil lamps somewhere but I doubt there's any oil.'

'How on earth do you get oil brought here?'

'You buys it in town and carries here,' Grenville said flatly.

'All the way down that track?'

'No, other way. Has to carry anything you want. Unless you got a donkey,' he chortled, revealing a row of yellow teeth. He was really quite a sinister looking chap. 'Alright. I'll leave you to it, then.'

He strode off into the night and Emma watched as he went back along the path. He must live somewhere the way she had come, though she hadn't noticed any other dwellings anywhere.

So this was it. It was nine-thirty, she was in a deserted cottage in the middle of nowhere, with the most basic of facilities. Her only light was provided by a box of candles which weren't going to last very long unless she rationed herself. She put some of them out. She picked up one of the candles and carried it carefully up the narrow stairs, shading the flame with her hand to prevent it blowing out.

There was no carpet and the bare boards echoed as she went up. It was horribly spooky. There seemed to be two bedrooms and nothing else up there. Iron bedsteads held lumpy looking mattresses but there was no bedding. It smelt damp and musty and certainly provided nowhere to sleep that night. Nor was there any sign of sanitation.

She hoped there was some sort of toilet somewhere. Probably outside.

Her candle would never stay alight in the wind that seemed to be howling outside suddenly. She took her little torch out through the back door and shone it round. There was a shed up the garden path. She looked inside and saw a wooden seat with a hole in it.

'Primitive or what?' she grumbled to no-one. But, if it was all there was, she'd just have to make the best of it and, grimacing slightly, she used it. Spiders scuttled by at the light of her torch and she shivered. She had never minded spiders until now but the whole situation was making her nervous and jumpy. It was too late to do anything else now; she had to stay the night and tomorrow, she'd begin her search.

What could have happened to Charlie? It seemed clear that she had never been here. So where was she? Emma shivered. This was turning out to be a night she'd rather forget.

She took a candle into the living room and though dirty, saw what looked like a reasonable armchair. It would have to do. She took out several sweaters and a fleece from her case and tried to wrap herself in them and settled down. She could do nothing until daylight so she might as well try to sleep.

This was not exactly the start to the holiday that she'd been expecting. She'd been hoping for a nice meal, a bottle of wine and a long gossip, the two of them sitting cosily in front of a fire, talking late into the night.

She still felt cold. Perhaps it might be possible to light a fire. Or perhaps she could put the cooker on and drag the chair into the kitchen? But then, there might not be much gas in the cylinder and she could see no way of getting more down here. Perhaps Rob Grenville had been exaggerating or maybe he did own a donkey.

Emma tugged her clothes round her more tightly and closed her eyes, trying to make her surroundings go away. Every sound seemed to echo round the building and being an old place, creaks and groans seemed to be everywhere. Several times she got up and checked the doors were locked.

Exhausted, she finally dozed off a few times but was quickly awoken by the unfamiliar sounds and cramping in her muscles. The candle had burned down and she was left in darkness, trying to plan the best thing to do in the morning.

\*　　　\*　　　\*

Dawn finally lit the sky with distant vermillion streaks and Emma glanced at her watch. It was five-thirty and she peered out of the grimy windows.

The dim light revealed a thick mist was rising and she couldn't see anything beyond the garden. This nightmare was destined to continue for a while yet. She felt desperate for a cup of coffee but that was a dream she couldn't fulfil.

'Damn you, Charlie, where the hell are you? And why did I ever listen to you?'

The words echoed round the empty building with no curtains or carpets to absorb sound. Emma ran the tap at the sink and brown water gushed out. She ran it for several minutes until it became only fractionally less brown and finally splashed the icy water on her face, drying it on one of her t-shirts—she hadn't thought to bring even a towel, assuming Charlie would provide everything. Perhaps if she threw herself on Rob Grenville's mercy, he might at least give her a cup of coffee. She could ask him about the donkey too, she managed to giggle silently. If she was to stay on here, she needed to sort some basic provisions. Maybe there was a wheelbarrow somewhere? She could leave it at the top of the track while she went to buy things from somewhere and then wheel it back.

Emma went outside, sniffing the sea air and feeling the clean coldness going into her lungs. It felt good after the damp mustiness of the cottage.

The unkempt garden had no wheelbarrow or anything else remotely useful. It seemed everything had been cleared away apart from the most basic of furniture. She wondered who would have left it all so empty and desolate. If whoever had left the place to Charlie had actually been living there, what had happened to everything?

She heard a noise and faint sounds of voices. Someone was walking along the coastal path maybe. She went to the gate but the mist was covering everything and she could hear only muffled sounds and the faint noise of the waves breaking on the rocks far below. She went back inside and looked to see if there was any fuel to light a fire—at least it might air the place a little. There was nothing.

Every few minutes, Emma's mind went back to Charlie. Had something happened to her? She dialled the number again but there was still got no reply. She stood outside, listening intently but if there had been anyone near, they were there no longer. She heard the faint hum of an engine and peered towards where she thought the sea must be but the mist was too thick. Perhaps boats could get nearer and that might be the way of collecting supplies.

Thoroughly spooked, Emma decided to risk going to see Rob Grenville. It was only six-thirty. Perhaps Rob was an early riser.

She left her things inside the cottage and set off to look for his house in the direction she had seen him leave.

The mist was giving everywhere a dampness that seemed to penetrate through to her very bones. She fantasised about cups of steaming

13

hot coffee, bacon and eggs. She was starving and hoped the man could offer her something to eat. She would gladly pay him if he would. Maybe he had a nice cheery wife who would produce an amazing breakfast.

Off to one side, she saw another small track and went down it towards a cottage not unlike Charlie's inheritance. It did have smoke coming from the chimney, which she felt was most likely a good sign—at least someone was up. She went up the weed covered path and knocked at the door, heard a scuffling noise and again what she believed to be muffled voices. After what seemed like several minutes had passed, the door opened.

'Thought it might be you,' Rob said gruffly.

'I wondered if you'd take pity on me and give me a cup of coffee, or tea? Better still could I buy some breakfast from you?'

He stared at Emma, a look of confusion crossing his face.

'Sorry. Got nothing in.'

'Just black coffee would do. I just need something hot to warm me.'

'You can't come in. Sorry.' He made to shut the door but she put her hand out.

'Please, if you can't give me even a drink, perhaps you can tell me where the nearest shop is?'

'If you walks back up to the main road, there's a garage a way along. They has a shop of sorts. Buses go along the road sometimes so you can get into town. You gonna leave then?'

'No,' she said firmly, suddenly deciding she needed to ask a few questions, if not of him, then of anyone else around. She would also go to the police and see if there had been an accident. 'I'm going to stay around and see if I can find out where Charlie is.'

'Not a good idea. You should get yourself back to where you come from. Get yourself gone. Or go and stay somewhere that would suit you better.'

She smiled sweetly at this strange man.

'You seem decidedly keen to get rid of me. Can you tell me the name of the solicitor who gave you the key to the cottage?'

'Don't know him. Didn't need no keys, any road. Place is always left open. Always has been. When Martha was alive, she never locked up. Now, I have work to do. Go away while you can,' he said ominously.

'Not sure what you mean by that,' she replied mustering what lightness she could. 'I'll see you around.'

*Miserable git,* she thought as she retraced her steps back to Gull Cottage. She would change her clothes and walk the ninety miles or whatever it was up to the main road. Civilisation couldn't be so far away, not in the twenty-first century.

15

# CHAPTER 2

By eight o'clock, Emma was walking along the main road looking for the garage, praying it would be open at this hour. She hoped it was one of those places with a coffee machine and better still, one that had sandwiches. She wanted to speak to someone about Bodilly Cove. It was certainly off the beaten track but surely in these days, it wasn't totally isolated from civilisation. Rob Grenville was doing his best to put her off. Maybe he hoped to buy the place himself for some purpose or other. Weird guy.

It was with relief that she saw the large signs hanging over the garage. And better still, the shop was just opening.

'Morning,' she said to the cheerful looking woman. What a relief it was to see someone looking happy.

'Morning dear. You're an early bird. How can I help?'

'Do you have a coffee machine?' Emma asked. 'I'm desperate for a hot drink.'

'There's one in the garage waiting area. You know, where folks sit while they're waiting for their cars to be serviced. Are you alright? You look very pale.'

'I've had a bit of a bad experience, really.' Unable to stop herself, she poured out the

16

sorry saga of the previous night. 'And Rob wouldn't even give me a cup of coffee.'

'Doesn't surprise me at all. Look, you get together the bits of shopping you need and I'll go and fetch you a coffee. How do you like it?'

'Just with milk if there is some. Hot and wet anything will do me fine, actually. Thank you so much.'

The woman went through the back of the shop into the garage. Emma picked up a wire basket and collected a few things from the well stocked shelves. Coffee, milk powder—better than fresh milk this warm weather with no fridge—bread and butter and a pack of ham. She spotted candles and torch batteries and added those to the basket.

'I'm Lucinda,' the woman said as she came back with two large cups of coffee. 'Thought I'd treat myself while I'm at it. Got some stuff together, have you?'

'Actually, I might just leave it here for now. I really need to get something to eat now but then I think I should go into Penzance. See if I can solve some of these mysteries that are surrounding this trip. Do you know when the buses go?'

'First one's at nine. You could always hire one of our cars if you want to travel around a bit. And if you wait another half hour, our fresh pasties will be delivered. One of them should keep you going for a while.'

Finishing what was possibly the best cup of

17

coffee she had ever drunk, Emma nodded.

'Maybe hiring a car would be a good idea. Though I can't get very near the cottage, at least it goes part way down the track. Save the walk down the lane, too. What have you got available in the way of hire cars?'

'You'd have to ask Harry. We keep a few oldish models to loan to people having services.'

'Thank you. You've been very kind. It's nice to know there are a few cheery people around here.'

'Bless you, dearie. You don't want to take no notice of Rob Grenville. He's always got some deal going somewhere. Few sandwiches short of a picnic, if you get my meaning.'

'Doesn't have a wife?'

'Bless you, no. Nobody'd cope with living with him and his funny ways.'

'But I could have sworn I heard voices when I knocked on the door this morning.' Was that a flicker of something that crossed Lucinda's face, or was it just Emma's imagination?

'No dear, you're mistaken. Rob lives there on his own, quite alone. Now, if you're hoping to get this car sorted, you'd best go and speak to Harry afore he gets busy.'

The woman seemed a little less friendly all of a sudden, as if she hadn't liked what Emma said. Maybe Emma was imagining things. Her nerves were stretched to breaking point after the night she'd just spent.

18

'Only got an old Fiesta spare today, but she's a sound runner and you can have her cheap for a couple of days,' Harry told her. 'Just need to see your driving licence and take your address.'

Emma fumbled in her bag and produced the licence.

'Lovely. Now your address?'

'What, home address or where I'm staying?'

'I'll have both. Not much use having your home address when you're staying down here.'

Emma gave both and when she mentioned Gull Cottage, Bodilly Cove, Lucinda looked up at her.

'What you doing down there, dear? Place is in near ruins. Not a good place to be.'

'I know, but it's where I am. My friend has inherited it and was supposed to be here but she's gone missing. I need to sort things out and find out what's happened. She sent me a postcard with a picture from here so she must have arrived. It's all a mystery.'

'Right then. Sign here and I'll get you the keys. You can give me the deposit on your credit card if you like,' Harry said. He, too had completely changed when he knew where she was staying. What was going on? It was as if everyone resented a stranger coming into the area, but that was ridiculous. It was a holiday area and early July was just the start of the holiday season, surely?

Emma went back into the shop and bought

one of the hot pasties, then sat outside and ate it as if it was the first meal she'd had in weeks, never had anything tasted that good. She wiped her mouth and went back inside the shop.

'Do you know where the nearest point is that you can get down to the cottage? I can't believe there's no way to get nearer than that parking place at the top.'

'I'm not sure. There's a farm somewhere that might have access but I'm not saying it'd help. You're in for a time of it if you stay there, believe me,' Lucinda told her.

'Well, thanks very much for your help—and the coffee and the pasty. Best thing I've eaten in ages. I'll see you again later to collect my shopping.'

\*       \*       \*

The mist had lifted and the sun was breaking through as Emma drove the few miles towards Penzance, following the signs to the town centre. She parked in a large car park overlooking the harbour and looked for a map of the area. The police station was in the middle of the town and she walked along sunlit streets, feeling as if she was miles away from the nightmare of Gull Cottage.

Several cafes and coffee shops spilled tables out on the street and she sat down at one, trying to decide what she would say at the

20

police station.

Perhaps she should try to find the solicitor who had been dealing with Charlie's inheritance? It must surely be a local practice if the deceased was an old lady living locally. But, it was probably unlikely anyone would give her any information in these days of security and proving one's identity for the least excuse. No, the police station was her best bet.

She drank the last of her coffee and set off to look for the police station.

'I want to enquire about a friend of mine who seems to have gone missing,' she said the officer behind the desk. He was quite young and rather nice looking.

'How long has she or he been missing? And you're sure they are really missing, not just gone on holiday?'

'Well yes. She was coming down to Cornwall last Saturday and I was joining her yesterday, but she didn't turn up to collect me, and evidently, she never arrived at her cottage. At least, that's what I was told, but I got a postcard from her and it was posted from here, which suggests she did actually arrive.'

'The name of your friend?'

'Charlie . . . Charlotte Danvers.'

He wrote it down. 'Did you say she has a cottage down here somewhere then?'

'Yes. Gull Cottage at Bodilly Cove.'

The officer looked up. Once more, the name of the place seemed to provoke a reaction from a local person.

'Bodilly Cove? Not a good place,' he said.

What was going on? Everyone seemed to think it was a bad place and even the name seemed to have a strange effect on people— even a police officer.

'She inherited it recently. We're supposed to be having a holiday there, but the place is empty and practically stripped of furniture. Do you know anything about it? Why does everyone think it's such a dreadful place.'

'It's got a bad reputation. It was once the home of a notorious smuggler. They say there are caves beneath it and a tunnel going down to the sea, somewhere in the garden.'

'Oh, for goodness sake! Surely that's all fantasy? Smugglers and pirates went out years ago. I'm sorry but I don't buy it. People are just trying to frighten me off. Maybe someone hopes to buy it cheap and make a holiday home out of it.'

The officer glared at her and gave a sigh. 'Have it your own way. What's the name of your friend, again?' He began to fill in a form, looking distinctly grumpy. 'Number and make of the car you say she was driving.'

'Sorry, I can't remember the number. It's a couple of years old and bright yellow. Some sort of Mini I think. Sorry. It's just a yellow car to me.'

'Mini Cooper, perhaps?'

'Probably. It has a black roof, a convertible,

I think.'

'Right. I'll check our records and see if there's anything remotely like it with any notices about it.'

He tapped various things into a computer and watched the screen. He blanched visibly and looked up at her. 'When did you say she was driving down?'

'Last Saturday. July the seventh.'

'And when did you get the postcard. In fact, have you got it with you?'

Emma produced it from her bag and handed it over. He looked at the picture and the message and then the postmark. He looked very uncomfortable.

'What is it? What have you seen?'

'Just give me a minute, Miss, I need to check something.'

He went into the back of the reception area and spoke to someone sitting at a desk. He looked up at her and nodded. The officer came back, a serious expression on his face.

'Would you like to come through? I'll take you into one of the interview rooms. One of our more senior officers will come through to talk to you.'

'What's going on? For goodness sake, what do you know?'

'Come through please. Do you want some tea?'

'No thanks. I've just had a coffee. Please can you tell . . .'

He led her through a door and into a corridor where several doors opened off it. He showed her into a plain, anonymous looking room with a table and chairs and a large recording machine to one side. It felt like some TV drama and she was the criminal being interviewed.

A man and woman came into the room.

'Miss Peterson?' The man spoke first.

'Yes. I'm Emma Peterson. What's going on? Is there some news about my friend?'

'I'm Sergeant Davies and this is Constable Thomas. There may be some news to give you. Were you—are you—very close to Charlotte Danvers?'

'Well yes. We've been friends since school. You said *were* you—what do you mean?' Emma shivered.

'I'm afraid I have some very bad news for you. Your friend has been killed in a car crash. We're not sure what exactly happened but the car was completely burnt out. She couldn't have suffered, she must have died instantly. I know that isn't any comfort to you.'

'Have you told her parents?' Emma felt unbelievably calm, as if the enormity of their words hadn't penetrated her consciousness.

'We haven't managed to trace them.'

'Oh, they live abroad. Spain somewhere.'

'That explains it. Thank you. I suppose you don't know where in Spain?'

Emma shook her head. Charlie dead? Of

24

course she wasn't. Someone of twenty-five didn't die just like that.

'Can I see her?' she asked suddenly. It was the only way she could believe their words. It wouldn't be too difficult to look at a body because it wouldn't be Charlie. It would be some other poor family's loss.

'I'm afraid not. I'm sorry but she is totally unrecognisable. The body was completely burned.'

A picture of charred remains, like in a television drama, flashed through her head.

'So, how do you know it's her?'

'The car, it was registered to your friend. It all points to it being Charlotte.'

'I don't see how. Not if you can't recognise anything.'

'I know it's difficult to grasp. There was the remains of a bag that somehow survived the blaze. It dropped out of the back when the floor of the car fell away. Part of her name is written on it in giant letters. It tied in with the registration number that we could decipher.'

'I know the bag. She drew it on so she could easily find it when it came through the airport carousel.' The tears started to fall as Emma was slowly coming to believe the officers' words. 'Where did the accident happen?' Her voice was hoarse.

'It was on the A30, just north of Penzance.'

'And when was it?'

'Saturday night, about nine o'clock. She

must have been on her way down here.'

'I really can't believe it. No, that can't be right. She was leaving very early on Saturday morning. She would have arrived in Cornwall early in the afternoon, at the latest.'

'I'm sorry. I know this is very distressing for you. Did she contact you at all on Saturday? I mean, do you know for a fact she arrived in Cornwall earlier in the day?'

'Well no, but the postcard. She couldn't have sent me a postcard that arrived on Wednesday. How could she have bought it and posted it if she was killed on Saturday?'

Emma felt relief sweep through her. It was obviously a mistake. The officers looked at each other.

'Perhaps she bought it and posted it on her way down.'

'But it's not a place where they sell loads of cards to tourists. Bodilly Cove is nowhere. The postmark says Monday, Monday the ninth. It reached me on the eleventh.'

'Well, maybe she put in a box that didn't have a weekend collection. If she posted it on Saturday after the post had been collected, it wouldn't have left 'till Monday.'

'But she must have bought it in the local shop. It's a Penzance postmark. I've never seen this picture anywhere else.'

'Look, you need to take a little time to let it sink in. I'm really sorry for your loss. I'll get some tea organised and you can sit quietly for a bit. Then perhaps you can make a statement so we have part of the picture completed.'

'Is there any way I can find out who dealt with her inheritance? I mean some local solicitor must know something about this cottage.'

'I'm afraid we can't really help you with that information. Perhaps you can set things out as far as you know them when you feel ready to make a statement. If we find out anything relevant when we make our enquiries, we'll let you know.'

'I need some air,' Emma said suddenly. 'I'm think I'm going to faint.'

'I'll come outside with you,' said the woman officer who had spoken very little. 'A little walk might help. You've had a terrible shock but you're being very brave.'

'I'm not being brave at all. I just feel frustrated that you won't see that it can't be Charlie.'

'I know it's hard to take it in, but it is her car and we think the driver was female.'

'How can you tell?'

'Various reasons.'

'What about DNA testing? Have you done that?'

'I'm sorry but I can see you're in complete denial. Let's get some air and then we'll see if you're up to making a statement.'

Emma stood up but found her legs didn't seem to want to react in their normal way. She staggered slightly and held onto the table for a moment. The female officer helped steady her and led her outside the police building to the rear, where there were a couple of benches.

There, she slumped down on one of them and tried to breathe more deeply. She tried to get her head round all of this. This was some sort of ridiculous nightmare and she'd wake up soon and find herself back in her home in the Midlands. Charlie was too vital, too lively not to come bouncing round the corner any minute, laughing and saying she'd forgotten the time.

After some while, Emma got up and went back inside. Tears refused to come and she felt cold and dead inside. The nightmare of the cottage was nothing compared to this.

She wondered who owned it now, if Charlie really was dead. Was she even entitled to stay there? Perhaps she should turn tail and go back home, let someone else sort out everything. But there was something deep inside that was telling her she needed to stay and there were too many things that were not quite right.

'Do you feel up to making a statement? Just a short one?'

'OK, but I'm not sure what I can tell you.'

She went through her story again, the policewoman writing it all down carefully. She confirmed the timing as far as she knew it and described Charlie's car and even the

28

travel bag.

'Can I see it?' she asked.

'It might upset you to see what's left of it but yes, if you like.'

The man left the room and returned carrying a plastic bag with the fragments of a burnt travel bag. Charlie's name, or the ragged remains of it, was clearly there.

Emma felt the tears begin to flow at last and she sobbed as if it would never stop. The police officers left her alone for a while, pushing a box of tissues towards her. They brought her some tea and the woman put a kindly hand on her shoulder.

'Come on now. It's good you cried but you need to drink this and then decide what you're going to do next. Do you want me to recommend somewhere for you to stay?'

'I need to go back to the cottage. All my things are there. I'll pick up a few more things in the town and go back there at least for tonight,' Emma said.

'It's a bit of a lonely place, cut off from everywhere. I'm not sure you should be left alone, not after this shock.'

'I'd prefer to be on my own. I'd like to drive a bit closer to the cottage though. Do you know if there's any way down there?'

'Hang on. I'll ask Sam if he knows. He lives that way and knows the cliff path like the back of his hand.'

She went out and came back with the desk

officer, who was carrying a detailed map.

'The farm at the top of the lane had a track down their fields. I'll give him a call for you and see if he'll let you drive over his fields. It's pretty dry at the moment so it should be safe enough. See, this is the coastal path along here, below the cottage. The little track leading to your cottage goes off the path just above it,' he said, pointing it out on the map. 'This is the farmer's field. Your cottage is the other side of the hedge, just here.'

'Gosh, that would be wonderful. I want to collect some provisions and some paraffin for the oil lamps and I didn't fancy carting it all that way down the track. I wonder why Rob didn't tell me about this?'

'Rob Grenville? He's an awkward cuss at the best of times. Hates anyone being within five miles of him, I reckon. Usually up to no good. I'll go and make the call.'

Emma sat waiting while the statement was being typed.

Sam came back and smiled. 'Mr Crelly says he doesn't mind you driving down his field, as long as you don't let a whole load of people follow you. And please shut the gates behind you. He doesn't want his stock to get out.'

'Thank you very much. I'm grateful.'

'You still sure you want to be there on your own?'

'I think so. A bit of light around the place and some fires to air it. And I can get some food in. I think I'll be fine.'

She stifled a sob as she thought again about her friend.

# CHAPTER 3

Emma walked back the car park, looking at the shops as she went. There were racks of postcards outside many of them and she glanced to see if there were any like the one Charlie had sent. So many pictures of all the various places around but none of Bodilly Cove.

She went to one of the large supermarkets and bought a whole load of things. As well as food, she collected cleaning materials, a sleeping bag and a supply of candles, batteries and a camping lantern. She picked up a cheap picnic set, with plates, mugs and cutlery packed in a shrink wrap pack. She also bought a small gas camping stove in case there was no gas left in the cylinder at the cottage.

Somehow, concentrating on such practicalities took away the need to believe terrible news about Charlie. She needed something more to believe it. Though the police had kept the postcard, she simply did not believe in the accident and wanted to look at it again. Feeling a light sense of obligation to the garage and shop, she went back there and bought a few more items from Lucinda.

'Any luck with finding out about your friend?' Lucinda asked, still cheerfully smiling.

'It's terrible news. They say she's been killed in a car accident, but I find it hard to believe. The timing doesn't fit and I had a card from her, apparently posted after the accident was supposed to have happened. Do you sell cards with pictures of Bodilly Cove?'

'I think we do have a few. They're not exactly popular like most of the well known places. Have a look over on the rack.'

'Thanks.'

Emma looked at the small range. A picture identical to the one she had received was there. Only two were left, slightly battered looking, so she picked them up and added them to her shopping basket.

'I think that's the lot.'

Lucinda checked the items through the till. 'You're not staying on, I take it?' she said. 'You can't stay on in that awful place with the terrible news you've had.'

'I think I have to, for now. I can't believe it's true and I have to try to find out more. I'll be alright. I'm quite tough these days. Have to be.'

'Well, pop in again and keep me posted.'

'I will. Thank you.'

As she drove down the lane, Emma kept a look out for the farm entrance—there it was on the right-hand side. She had somehow missed it before when she was walking up the lane in the other direction. She turned into the drive and up to the farmhouse, where she knocked on the door.

A large woman came out, wiping her hands on a spotlessly clean towel. 'Can I help you?'

'I think someone from the police station called you to ask if I might drive through your field and leave my car at the bottom near the cottage. Gull Cottage. I'm staying there.'

'Oh yes, Sam phoned. You're welcome to use our track as long as you shut the gates and don't let just anyone use it.'

'I'm very grateful. Sam told me about shutting the gates.'

'I hear there was a terrible accident. The girl who was supposed to be moving there.'

'Well, yes. So I understand. I take it you didn't see anything of her? She was supposed to be here on Saturday.'

'No dear, I saw nothing. But I didn't think she ever arrived here, did she?'

'I'm not sure. Everyone seems to think she didn't get here but she sent me a postcard. It was posted after she was supposed to have died. I just can't believe it.'

'Maybe it was put in one of those boxes that never got collected 'till the Monday.'

'I don't understand. She must have been somewhere near here to have bought that particular picture. They don't seem to sell them anywhere else.'

Emma was getting weary with trying to sell her theory but people were listening with a look in their eyes as if they knew she was clutching at straws.

'Sorry, I'm keeping you from your work,' she murmured.

'That's alright. Look, you can phone us if you have any problems. My husband's usually out in the fields but I'm mostly around. I assume you've got a mobile phone?'

'Well yes, thank you. I'm not sure how long the battery will last though. Not having electricity makes it difficult.'

'Bring it in here if you need to. You can leave it to charge if you go out somewhere.'

'You're very kind. Thank you.'

'And you can always have a few of our eggs and some milk when you need it.'

Emma was so touched she almost burst into tears. 'Thank you. You're the first person I've met who's actually offered help of any sort.' She gave a stifled snort.

'I take it you've met Rob Grenville, then?'

'I asked him for a cup of coffee this morning but he shooed me away as if I was poison.'

'Take no notice of him. He's usually up to some nefarious deal or other. They say he's doing some smuggling on a small scale and doesn't welcome any visitors at all. Probably sees you as a threat.'

'Maybe. It wasn't a very nice welcome though. I take it the track is easy to follow?'

'Go through the first field and then take the second gate at the bottom, on the left, then you follow it down. There are a few heifers in the field but they won't hurt you. Bit curious they are, but don't worry. Nothing in the next field. You park by the hedge. There's a wooden fence you can climb through quite easily.'

'Thanks again. I'll see you later.'

Emma drove carefully down the rutted track, usually used by a tractor rather than a narrower wheeled fiesta. When she stopped to open the gate, the heifers—or just cows as she'd have called them—came close to the car and she nervously shooed them away. She'd never been quite this close to them before and despite Mrs Crelly's assurances, she wanted to remove herself from them as soon as possible.

She could see the roof of the cottage as she drove down the field and parked at the bottom. There was a gap in the hedge with a wooden fence topped with barbed wire. She unloaded the car and put the shopping over the fence so she only once had to climb through herself.

As Emma walked down the path, the gloom began to submerge her mind again. It was truly a miserable place and the reactions of many of the people she had met, seemed to add to the grim nature of the whole area. She simply could not believe her friend, the vibrant and lovely girl who was Charlie, could be dead.

What did everyone say? You needed something positive to provide closure. People who lost relatives at sea were always hoping they might return. Closure was a phrase she had never really taken on board until now, but she needed undisputable proof that it had been Charlie in that car.

She went inside the cottage and dumped the shopping on the kitchen table. She planned to clean a bit of the kitchen area so she could use it. Then she needed to find some firewood to get fires going. Despite the warm day and sunshine that had broken through, the house felt damp and cold.

Was it worth the effort? It would probably be more sensible if she simply gave up and went home, but she felt some deeper obligation to follow things through. She went into the sitting room where she had left her luggage. Had she left it quite like that? There were some things taken out that she didn't realise she had moved.

Looking round, she felt certain someone had been in here and moved things, but she had locked up before she had left and taken the key with her. Perhaps Rob still had a key to the place and had been searching through her things. She shuddered. She hated the thought of anyone handling her stuff, especially him, Rob Grenville.

Maybe it was her over stimulated imagination running wild again. Gritting her teeth, she set to work.

Emma carried the armchair outside and struggled to get one of the mattresses from the bed down the stairs put out to air in the warm sun. She opened windows and cleaned the sink, the cooker and scrubbed the table, then wiped out the cupboards to put her food in. She had even bought a small saucepan so she could boil some water to make coffee.

It was late into the afternoon by the time she was satisfied she had done all she could to make conditions marginally habitable. She heated up a can of soup and put cheese and salad onto a plate. She took them to the doorstep and sat in the sun to eat her simple meal.

Once she relaxed, her mind was once more troubled by the terrible visions of Charlie, the lovely girl possibly destroyed by fire, but still she couldn't or wouldn't accept it.

Emma heard someone coming along the path and stiffened. It wasn't the actual coastal path below the cottage and no holiday makers would normally be using it. She didn't feel like another encounter with Rob and leaned back into the doorway so she couldn't be seen.

'Hello there,' called a male voice. 'Miss Peterson?'

Emma rose to look. If it was someone who knew her name, it shouldn't be a problem.

'Hello?' she called tentatively.

'I just thought I'd come and see if you are

alright.' It was Sam, the desk officer from the police station, dressed in a T-shirt, shorts and trainers.

'Goodness, that was kind of you.'

'I live at a cottage a bit further along. The next village as the crow flies. I was having a run along the path so thought I'd divert and call on you, just make sure all is well.'

'I'm sort of alright. Still pretty shocked and disbelieving.'

'I'm sorry. Do you want to talk or am I upsetting you?'

'I'd like to talk. Can I get you some coffee? It's a bit primitive inside but I got a camping stove and a saucepan. I'm assuming the water is safe once it's been boiled.'

He followed her inside.

'There's a spring that feeds your supply. Old Martha survived to a ripe old age so I expect it's OK. Interesting, I never knew she had any family. Your friend must have been a distant cousin or something.'

'I suppose so. What happens to this place now?'

'No idea. I suppose your friend's parents will inherit it,' he replied. 'Are you sure you'll be alright here? It's all pretty basic.

I imagine the bedrooms are damp too.' He looked around.

'I've had a mattress outside airing all afternoon.'

'Do you need help getting it back in?'

'Well, yes please. That will save me struggling with it. Thanks . . . er, Sam. Sorry, I don't know your other name. Someone said your name was Sam at the police station.'

'Sam's fine, though it's Sam Henley, just for the reference.'

'I'm Emma.'

'OK Emma, let's get you more comfortable. Where did you sleep last night?'

'Didn't exactly sleep. I sort of sat on that horrible chair. I feel exhausted now, so I hope I can get some sleep tonight. I kept hearing noises and then it sounded like a crowd of people walking past the gate.'

He looked at her sharply. 'Really? When was that?'

'Must have been around five or five-thirty this morning. It was really thick mist so I thought I must have been dreaming.'

'And did you hear any other sounds?'

'Apart from the creaking and groaning of an old cottage? Not really. Oh, I did think I might have heard a boat engine in the distance. Or it could have been a plane somewhere overhead. It was hard to tell with the mist. Sounds seem distorted.'

'Interesting. Something we may investigate at some point.'

They sat outside on the step for a while, sipping coffee and chatting comfortably. Every now and again, the memory of the true situation hit her.

'I still can't believe it was Charlie in that car,' she said.

'So who else could it have been?'

'Suppose someone stole it and it was them driving it?'

'Wouldn't she have reported it? Charlie, I mean of course. And where would she have gone in the meantime? You're clutching at straws.' He paused and looked at her with a worried expression on his face. 'Shouldn't you consider going home?'

'I can't leave things like this. Do you think they'd let me see the car? I might recognise something to make it more certain?'

'I'll let you know. Have you got a mobile number?'

Emma gave him her number and he put it in his phone.

'Would you like my private number? Then at least you'll have a friend nearby. Unofficially of course.' He smiled warmly.

'Some people are very kind. Mrs Crelly at the farm was very nice and Lucinda at the garage.'

'Not everyone's like Rob Grenville, you know.'

'But I don't understand why everyone grimaces when I say I'm staying here. They say things like it's a bad place.'

'It has a reputation. Martha died rather suddenly. We did look into it, as we always do with sudden death, but she was in her eighties, so the verdict was misadventure. She'd put the oven on and then must have slipped when she bent down to light it. She banged her head and unfortunately, the gas overcame her. She was here on her own, as always.'

'What a terrible end. Poor lady. But you say there was nothing suspicious about it?'

'Not really. There was a dish of food in the oven so it seemed more than likely it happened the way I just told you.'

'Goodness, old age is scary.'

'Not just old age. Now, let's get this mattress back for you.' They heaved it up the narrow stairs. Emma was most grateful and realised she would never have managed it on her own.

Sam looked around. 'It's pretty depressing up here. I wonder what happened to Martha's stuff? She had some nice pieces.'

'She must have left it to someone. Or maybe it was sold to cover expenses. Expect the lawyers took it to settle the will.'

'No, she was actually surprisingly well off, considering. Her expenses were very small and she left quite a tidy sum. I don't know who the money was left to or where it originated. We mostly turned a blind eye to what might have been going on. I suspect she allowed access to the tunnel for a spot of smuggling, you know.'

'So what do people smuggle these days? I can hardly imagine casks of brandy or the likes being needed.'

'You'd be surprised. Quite a bit of cheap

41

booze comes in. Mainly it's drugs and tobacco. They do land quite a bit of fish too. With restrictions and quotas, small fishermen often sell their catches on the black market. There's a fish processing place a couple of miles further on. They do stuff like crab picking and a few lobsters find their way to local restaurants.'

'Goodness. I'd never have thought any of that would be worthwhile. Drugs, maybe. I know it's a problem everywhere. But fish?'

'That why we haven't really followed anything up. With all these Common Market restrictions, one can't help but have some sympathy. Can't imagine Martha actually earning millions, but she obviously got something out of it.'

'If she had money, I wonder why she didn't have the place modernised a bit? Get electricity put in or at least a generator.'

'She'd never experienced electricity so never missed having it, I suppose. She used to get supplies delivered to the farm and the Crellys brought it down or she walked up to collect it. She was a nice old lady, quite a character. I miss her in a way. Used to stop off for a cuppa with her occasionally. And she was quite friendly with my mum.'

'Maybe the furniture got nicked. Rob said he used to come and go in the place when she was alive. He must have known what was here. I suppose it's not really anything to do with me. I'm not even sure I should be staying here without Charlie.'

'I shouldn't worry. But I am concerned about you. It's pretty remote and you've had a terrible shock today. But you do seem remarkably calm.'

'Because I don't believe what you're telling me.'

'Well, if you're sure. I'd better go. Mum'll think I've got lost.'

'You live with your parents, do you?'

'Just Mum. Dad died a couple of years ago so I moved back to be with her. I did have a flat in Penzance. I don't mind though. I like it here and I'm saving money.'

'Well, thanks again for your concern. I'll be in touch.'

Emma watched as he walked away and then began to run again. He turned to wave and she waved back.

She felt very alone again and the demons started to curl into her mind. She tried to push them away and went inside to stoke up the fire. She shut all the windows, even though it was now warm inside the house, locked the door and dragged the chair in front of the door. If anyone did have a key and tried to get in during the night, they'd never make it.

Exhausted from the lack of sleep the previous day, Emma settled down early, but she slept fitfully, her thoughts surfacing from time to time into a waking nightmare.

'She isn't dead . . . Charlie isn't dead . . .' she told herself again and again.

Emma dozed once more but was woken by strange noises. She hugged the sleeping bag around her as she imagined mice, or worse still, rats scuttling above her head. She shivered and tried to tell herself it was imagination but the noises persisted. This whole thing was a crazy idea. She needed to give up and find somewhere sensible to stay, have a proper holiday and get over the death of her friend and go back home.

But she'd come away to try and forget her own problems of the past weeks and decide about the future. When she went back, it was going to be a completely new start. Her first task would be to find a new job, get right away from Preslight and Company. And Anthony.

You couldn't be with someone for eight years, get engaged, arrange the wedding and then stay in the same company, while watching him with his new love. Only one week before their wedding, he had announced that he'd fallen in love with someone else. Worse, the woman was pregnant with his child.

Emma tried to push the thoughts from her mind; there were more pressing matters to deal with first.

\*       \*       \*

At least when dawn finally broke, she could get up and make coffee today. Her basic supplies were enough to keep her going for a while and in daylight, everything seemed more manageable. She would explore the cove and possibly look for this mysterious tunnel the smugglers were supposed to use.

It was already quite light and when the sun rose, the sky became a wonderful deep pink colour, streaked with gold. It was stunningly beautiful. She made a sandwich and sat on a rock at the bottom of the garden, looking out over the azure sea. If her mind wasn't quite so crazy, she could have appreciated the beauty of the place much more.

Dominating all her thoughts was the need to find out what had really happened last Saturday. She would start with the garage. Someone must remember if they had sold one of the last few postcards showing Bodilly Cove. Emma cursed herself for not asking Lucinda yesterday and went back inside and took out the two postcards she had bought. She stood looking down at the sea and rocks below and worked out the very point at which the picture must have been taken.

It was obviously an old picture, the card slightly faded and yellowing, but the scene had barely changed at all. The bushes were taller but everything else was just the same. It was an amazing throwback, considering the way most places were overdeveloped these days. A time capsule with a view that must have been the same for possibly thousands of years. Emma peered along the path further towards the east, wondering if she could see any other buildings but the cliffs got in the way.

Back inside the cottage, she decided to try and wash as best she could. The water was icy cold but at least she felt better and, with a change of clothes, was more prepared for the day.

She decided to walk down to the sea and clear the fuzz out of her mind. Clean sea air might help her get her thoughts into some sort of order. She locked up and set off down the steep climb that linked up to the coastal path after a few yards. She crossed it and continued to walk down the narrow opening down and down until she reached the tiny bay itself.

It was truly beautiful. Unspoilt and picturesque, it was everyone's dream of an ancient, Cornish cove. The dark rocks surrounded the stony beach and cliffs towered high above, surrounding and sheltering the small inlet. In fact, there were several inlets, she realised. Narrow passages between the rocks that were just large enough to let a boat slide in to moor. Though the sun had risen above the cliffs behind, deep shadows were still covering the beaches giving and slightly forbidding look to the area.

Her feet crunched on the small pebbles at the top of the beach and she made her way to the sea's edge. She dipped her hand into the icy waters and decided she would not be going for a swim any time soon. She sat on a rock, contemplating the scene. She and Charlie would have sat here for ages, talking things through. Tears filled her eyes as she began to feel the loss afresh. Even if it wasn't a permanent loss, it was another day of her holiday that she was missing her friend's company. She tried to keep herself focussed on her disbelief but nagging doubts crept in from time to time.

Emma turned, bracing herself to tackle the steep climb back. She noticed a cave leading into the cliff face and went towards it. She almost laughed as she asked herself if this could be the entrance to the infamous tunnel. It certainly went a long way back and she wished she had brought her torch with her. There was a damp seaweed smell but the floor was quite dry. Perhaps the sea only came right inside when there was a storm or extremely high tide. If there was a way out at the back of the cave, she wasn't about to try and find it without light of some sort. She would come back later with her torch.

But now, it was time to go back and ask Lucinda if she knew of any purchasers of the postcard.

# CHAPTER 4

Emma was panting hard by the time she reached the top of the cliff. It was warm and sunny and she realised she was quite out of condition. When she let herself into the cottage, she once more got the feeling that someone had been inside while she was out. It was most disconcerting. Nothing was missing but it felt as if things had been disturbed. Small things, like clothes left on a chair where she hadn't put them. The dishes in the sink looked as if they were arranged differently. She looked in the food cupboard and could have sworn that the cheese pack had been opened and a piece removed.

But what could she do? Short of changing the locks or putting a padlock on the place, it was not really her place to do anything like that. Nor did she feel up to tackling Rob Grenville. He was far too unfriendly and almost sinister. The less she had to do with him the better.

She assumed it must be him as he was the only other person nearby. Under different circumstances, she might think of setting some sort of trap but right now, she had other things on her mind.

Emma climbed through the fence and got into the hire car then drove up the field to the gate. When she saw the cows were at the other side, she opened the gate, drove through and quickly closed it again. They didn't seem to have noticed her. She laughed silently. Being afraid of some young cows was nothing compared to the other dramas in her life at present. She noticed someone standing by one of the barns and stopped.

'Mr Crelly? How do you do. I'm Emma Peterson. Thank you for letting me drive over your field.'

'That's alright m'dear. Bad business all round, this. You plannin' on staying long? Only rain's forecast and fields'll be getting muddy.'

'I'm not sure. I need to find out more about what happened. You see, I don't really believe it was Charlie in that car.'

'So the Missus said. You'm possibly clutchin' at straws, girl. Not as I blames you. Good luck to you, I say. You carry on using the track as long as you want.'

'Thanks very much. It's kind of you. I'll see you later.' She drove up the lane, grateful that she didn't have to face the long walk each time.

At the garage, Lucinda greeted her like an old friend. 'So, you've lasted another night, have you?'

'Seems like it. I wanted to ask if you sold one of those postcards, the ones of Bodilly Cove, on Saturday at any time?'

'I'm not usually in on Saturdays. Young Colin minds the shop on Saturdays. I'm only covering this weekend because he's off doing some surfing competition. My old man hates it when I'm out at weekends but he doesn't say no to the bit of extra cash now, does he?'

'Do you know where I can find him? Colin, that is.'

'He'll be back home this evening I suppose. Unless he's staying on for the drinkin', with his mates.'

'I really need to know. Is there any way you can tell? I mean do you make a note of sales or does the till record show it up?'

'Not really. Just shows as miscellaneous, but I doubt it really. You could see how old they looked when you got them yesterday. Don't think they've shifted in months. We never ordered more as nobody seems to want them.'

'Oh well, thanks anyway. It was just a long shot.'

'Aren't you having one of my pasties today? You look like you could do with feeding up. I don't suppose you can cook anything much down there.'

'I'm very tempted but I think I'd better resist. I have to go into town and I'll get something there later.'

'Mind you do. Don't like to think of you down there on your own. Not a healthy place, Bodilly Cove.'

'Why does everyone keep saying that?'

'Think it goes way back into the past. And there was always something strange about old Martha's demise. Strong as an ox she was, yet just keeled over and died, they said, but I don't think so. Weren't like her to fall down.'

'It was very sad to hear. And the place was stripped practically bare. What's the talk about her furniture? And I've also heard that she'd a fair bit of money put by somewhere.'

'Don't know nowt about any of that.' Emma could swear Lucinda looked a little shifty.

Maybe various locals had gone in and helped themselves; easy pickings once the place was empty. The reputation of the old looters and wreckers probably still held a bit of sway even today. Such things may have been in the blood, as they say.

'I'd best be getting on,' Emma said at last. She didn't want to lose the confidence of someone who could prove to be a rare ally. 'Nice to see you again.'

'And you, dearie. Take care of yourself.'

'Thanks.'

Emma left the little shop and drove towards Penzance. Being a Saturday, the road was busy and the town even more so. She found one of the last parking spaces and paid for a couple of hours on the ticket. As she walked up the narrow street, on impulse, she dialled Charlie's number. To her amazement, the familiar voice mail message played.

'Sorry, I must be busy doing something.

Leave a message.'

'Charlie? It's me, Emma. Call me back. Where are you?'

Shaking with relief, she rushed to the police station. A different officer was on duty. Pity, as she would have liked it to be Sam again.

'Hello. My name's Emma Peterson. I was in yesterday concerning my friend, Charlie Danvers. She was supposed to have been in an accident but I now have another reason to think it wasn't her in the car.'

'One moment please, Miss.' He typed her name into the computer. 'Oh yes, here we are. Do you want to tell me what you think you've found out?'

'I just called her mobile and the voice mail message came up. If she'd been burned to death, her mobile would have been burnt too. So how could it have been answered?'

'Maybe she didn't have the phone with her. Perhaps she'd left it at home.'

'She'd never do that. She was always permanently attached to her phone.'

'Maybe you dialled the wrong number,' he said unhelpfully.

'Oh come on, please. I know my friend's message and I know her voice. Here, I'll dial it again. Hear for yourself.'''

She dialled the number and handed her phone to the police officer. He stared at her blankly.

'Nothing. It's just silent.'

'What?' She listened. The phone sounded dead. 'I don't understand. It definitely rang before. I got her voice message. Really I did.'

'Maybe you were wanting to hear it so badly that you imagined it.'

'I know everyone seems to think I'm stupid and refusing to accept the truth, but I can't. Can I have my postcard back?'

'Postcard?'

'The one Charlie sent me last Monday. Three days after you insist she was dead. I've only found one place that sells them so she must have been in the area to have bought it. Hence she couldn't have died somewhere on the way down to Cornwall. The people I spoke to yesterday asked if they could keep it. I want it back, now. It's the last thing I received from her.'

'The officers who interviewed you yesterday are off duty today, I'm afraid. Can you come back on Monday?'

'I suppose so. And I also want to see Charlie's car. I know I can't see the remains of the person but at least let me see the car,' she demanded as firmly as she could.

'I can't authorise it. They haven't finished with it yet at forensics, you see. Again, you'll have to come back on Monday. I'm sorry not to be more helpful. I know this must be very distressing for you.'

'You have no idea. Just trying to get someone to listen to me is the worst part.

Sorry, I know it's not your fault. I'll come back on Monday. I don't suppose Sam is on duty?'

'It's his weekend off too.'

Emma turned away, almost in tears. She blinked them away fiercely; she daren't let herself cry or she might never stop. But that gave her a whole other day as well as the rest of today to occupy herself. She needed to ask questions, to get some answers and be rid of this desperate feeling there was something she didn't know. She stood outside the police station and dialled Charlie's number again, but the phone remained dead. Her friend's phone was well and truly switched off.

Back in the high street, Emma looked at the numerous cafes and decided to get a proper meal. Living on the food she could actually prepare in her primitive conditions was not going to be good for her long term. Even though she didn't really feel like eating, she knew she needed to keep her wits about her and stay healthy.

After her meal, she realised she needed to get back to her car before her time ran out—a parking ticket was the last thing she needed. She drove along the coast a little way, not really wanting to return to the desolate cottage. She would park somewhere and go for a walk, try to sort out her churning brain and get a proper plan of action organised.

\*        \*        \*

The sun was hot and Emma sat in a pretty little village and ate an ice cream. Holidaymakers were arriving at the start of school holidays and filling the narrow streets with excited chatter. This was Cornwall in the tourist season, towns bustling and happy. How different from her own circumstances.

Emma scolded herself. *You can't give in now. You have to get answers and stop mooning around.*

She would explore the cave she had seen and see if she could discover this famous tunnel. She should also have a good search around the cottage and see if the other end of it was somewhere inside the building. That might explain how someone had got inside when she was away. She needed a much more powerful torch, maybe even one of those wind-up ones. That way, she wouldn't run out of batteries or need to re-charge it. And she would buy a cheap radio of some sort, something to cheer the long evenings, and maybe a book too.

Back in Penzance, she stopped at the supermarket again. She bought her torch, a book and a battery radio, then added some fruit and some canned food to her basket and remembered she needed a can opener. Even the simplest of meals needed extra equipment. She even put in a bottle of wine and remembered to make sure it had a screw cap. She needed some sort of treat to see her through until Monday.

Emma noticed the petrol gauge was almost on empty as she reached the lane to Bodilly Cove and drove on to the garage, where she filled the tank halfway, not knowing how far she might need to drive nor how long she would stay. She saw a rack of newspapers outside the shop, picked one up then went inside.

'Oh there's a picture of your friend's car in the local paper. I don't know if you want to see it or if it might upset you,' Lucinda warned her.

'I'm going to see the real thing on Monday so it might help to prepare me. Do you have a copy?'

'Only my copy, but you're welcome to it. I've read it now.'

'Thank you, that's kind. Oh, do you know where Colin lives? You did say it was Colin on duty last Saturday?'

'Colin James, he is. Lives in Langton. Third in the row of cottages on the left. He might be back there this evening. Or he may be in here tomorrow. He's supposed to phone me this evening and let me know if he's still in the competition.'

'OK, thanks,' Emma said. 'Perhaps I'll drive to his house later and see if he can remember anything. Thanks again.'

'Bye dearie. Do take care of yourself. See

you again soon.'

Emma drove down the lane and repeated the trek across the fields, parking at the bottom and unloading her supplies over the fence. The cottage was cool, despite the heat of the day and she opened the windows to let in some fresh air and sunshine. It looked just as she had left it and she felt certain nobody had been in this time.

Unpacking her shopping, she stowed things away, then switched on the radio and cheerful music echoed round the empty rooms. It was a cheap and tinny sound but it was company and made her feel less alone. She made coffee and sat outside but she was putting off looking at the local newspaper, knowing she would have to face seeing Charlie's ruined car. Maybe she would leave that until the next day.

Though it had been a few days since she had seen any national news, nothing seemed to have changed in the world; still fighting in the Middle East, floods in the North of Great Britain, sportsmen arguing over what they had done or hadn't done. It made her realise that whatever disaster hit personally, it was an insignificant part of the world in general.

Suddenly Emma heard people walking along the path below her and looked over the lower hedge. People with rucksacks were strolling by, chatting happily. There were even the odd few visitors down in the cove, clambering over rocks. She wondered where they'd come from and kept looking around her, almost hoping the nice policeman, Sam, would come by again. She could ask him some questions—she had enough random thoughts flitting through her head, after all.

She tried ringing Charlie's number again but there was never an answering ring again since that first time. Could she have imagined it? She felt certain she hadn't.

Sea birds were screeching out their plaintive cries and bees were humming everywhere in the untidy garden. Fat thistles were bursting into purple crowns and brilliant flames of Montbretia spread orange patches of colour wherever they could take root. Wild purple buddleias hosted myriad showers of butterflies, adding even more of a sense of normality to the scene. Under any other circumstances, this place would seem idyllic, a sanctuary of peace, undisturbed and a refuge from a crazy world. With a deep sigh for all the things she felt she was missing, Emma went inside to make some supper. She poured a mug of wine and carried her meal outside again to enjoy the evening sun and try to relax.

Tomorrow, Emma told herself, she would explore the cave and possibly see the man who helped in the garage shop. She couldn't face driving out again to find him this evening since she felt totally exhausted. Hardly surprising after the emotional drain of the past couple of days. Only a couple of days? Already she seemed to have lived through her nightmare for weeks. With the radio to keep her company when she went to bed, she actually settled into a deep sleep.

\*       \*       \*

When Emma awoke next morning, the sun had already risen and she could see blue skies and clear blue sea through the tiny window. She felt restored, more positive and more able to face the day. It was a huge relief after all the miseries and melancholy. With a sunny day like this one in prospect, she didn't have to be so depressed.

She made a simple breakfast of the rolls she had bought the previous day and some jam. She had a craving for toast but there was no gas left in the cooker. Not surprising, if Martha had died leaving it on. She shivered and looked at the place on the floor where her end must have taken place. But it was just a piece of slate. There were no real ghosts.

She ate one of the oranges and with coffee to complete the meal, felt much more positive as she looked down at the cove and decided to walk down there and look into the huge cave. With the new torch, she might even see if this mythical tunnel existed. It felt distinctly Enid Blyton and Famous Five, she decided, like some childish tale of adventure and secret passages, but behind it all, there was the reality

59

of her missing friend and the mystery that surrounded it.

Emma put on her heavy trainers ready for the climb and packed her large shoulder bag with a bottle of water and the torch. She wouldn't leave anything valuable behind, in case the mystery visitor came in again. She thought of the old Bond movies where he stuck a hair across the door to see if it was still in place when he returned—but her hair was too short for such tricks, even if it would have worked. But she did wedge a tiny scrap of newspaper into the gap as she shut the door and locked it. It wasn't visible from the outside and would fall down if the door was opened. She smiled at her neurosis but felt pleased that she had done it.

As she walked down to join the coastal path, she heard her name being called and turned.

'Wait Emma. I came to see how you're doing.'

'Sam! Great to see you. Nice of you to think of me. I'm OK. Bought a few more things to make life more comfortable.'

'That's good,' he said as he approached her. 'I was worried about you being here on your own.'

'I'm quite self-sufficient in my own way. Much more so than I would have thought possible, really. I was going down to the cove. I want to explore the cave down there and see if I can find this mysterious tunnel that's

60

supposed to exist.'

'Mind if I tag along? Or do you want to be on your own?'

'I'd be delighted if you came with me, Sam. It'll be nice to have someone to talk to, although I might bore you rigid with my wild theories.'

'You still haven't accepted that Charlie's gone?'

'No, not at all. I rang her phone yesterday and actually got her voice mail message. That couldn't possibly happen if the phone had been burnt, could it? I went to the police station again yesterday but when he tried the number it was dead. Just minutes later after I'd tried it. He said I'd imagined it because I wanted it to happen so much.'

'It's possible, I suppose.'

'Don't phone companies have ways of seeing when calls were made? I mean, can't they check?'

'Well yes, but only if they have the proper authorisation.'

'But you could do that, couldn't you? The police, I mean.'

'You're clutching at straws, Emma. There's no real reason to check on it. We're pretty certain your friend is lost.'

'I can't accept it. There are too many doubts—for me anyway. I'm going to find the chap who was working in the garage shop last Saturday. Charlie had to have bought the card from there. It's the only place that sells those particular old pictures and it proves she was here.'

'If he can remember, of course.'

'Stop putting me off, Sam. I know I'm right.'

'Concentrate where you're putting your feet. This bit is rather steep and there are lots of loose stones.'

He led the way down, turning every few steps to make sure she was alright. It was rather nice, she thought. He held out a hand when it was particularly slippery and she took it gratefully. The path widened again and they walked side by side.

'So, what are you doing walking over here on a Sunday morning? Don't you have someone to be with?'

'Nope. I do have to be back for lunch, though or Mum will never forgive me. Sunday lunch is an institution in Cornwall. Actually, why don't you come back with me? Mum always cooks enough for a small army and she'd be delighted to meet you and tell you all about old Martha. They used to be friends.'

'Well, if you're sure. It sounds great, but I'd hate to impose.'

'It is a bit of a walk, if you're up for it.'

'If there's time. But we could always drive. I have the hire car, don't forget.'

'Let's see how we do. Did you park in the Crelly's field?'

'Yes. They're very kind. It means I have it

close to the cottage instead of parking at the top of the track.'

They reached the beach. The tide was low and all the rocks seemed abandoned by the waves, left high and dry. They walked towards the sea and Emma noticed there were some rusty, heavily corroded rings let into the rock near what must have been an inlet at high tide.

'They use them to moor the boats when they came in from fishing,' Sam explained.

'They?'

'People from the past who lived and worked here.'

'Crikey. Must have been a long walk, especially if they were carrying fish.'

'It's the only place to land for a quite a distance. It was usually the locals fishing for themselves, nothing commercial. Feeding the family really. They grew vegetables and fished the sea, a simple life.'

'And a spot of smuggling on the side maybe?'

'Probably. Some things are in the blood. I'm sure it goes on today. Like I said, it's drugs mostly, though we do wonder if the odd few immigrants find their way through here. You must have heard about the gang masters who employ desperate immigrants to work the farms? There was a big case about it a while back. Daffodil pickers and other stuff. We've also wondered about the fish processors I mentioned to you.'

'I heard about it on the news. You think it still goes on?'

'Probably. We're always on the lookout, as I said. Now, are we going to look in this cave? It's pretty large and rather dark.'

'I have a torch.'

'Wow. Were you a scout or guide by any chance?'

'No, but I came down here yesterday and realised I couldn't get far without a light. It's a wind up thing so the battery won't run out. Don't suppose it lasts long without being wound but it should work OK.'

They went into the cave and the damp, sea-weedy smell filled their nostrils. She shone her beam round the high walls, smooth and shiny at the base where the sea washed them at high tides. Green tails of seaweed hung down, leaving some of the rocks looking treacherously slippery. Odd patches of sand showed through the pebbles on the ground, as if waiting for a child to arrive to make sand pies.

They walked on towards the back. The torch flickered and went out and Emma wound the handle furiously until the light came back.

'Clever invention,' Sam remarked. 'Shine it to the left there. Is that a hole at the back?'

'It might be. I'll get closer and look.'

'Don't slip. I don't fancy carrying you back up the path.'

'Take care yourself, too. I doubt I could

64

even drag you out of the cave, let alone up the path. But I have my phone with me so I could always call for a helicopter.'

'You actually think you could get a signal down here?'

'S'pose not. Looks like this is a dead end. Does this tunnel actually exist or is it just an urban myth?'

'Coastal myth if anything. It's always been talked about since I was a kid but I've never seen it. Try further back.'

They went deeper into the cave. The roof was getting lower and Emma began to feel claustrophobic. The air felt stale. She shivered as the torch died again.

'I'll give it a wind if you like.' Sam took it and turned the handle like mad.

'I'm sorry but I don't like this,' Emma told him. 'Even if there's a tunnel further back, it must be pretty stale air. I think I'm ready to give up.'

'Fair enough. I suspect it's a lost cause anyway. We could look in the house or garden. Maybe the entrance is there.'

'Maybe. Shouldn't we go back anyway? By the time we've got back up to the top of the cliff, it'll be time to get to your place for this lunch you promised me. If you're sure your Mum won't mind.'

'I'll call when we get back up there, just to make sure, but I know she'll be delighted.'

They turned back and walked towards the

entrance, taking care not to slip on the smooth stones. It was better walking towards the light.

Emma paused and shone the torch to one side where she saw something red between two rocks and went over to look. It was probably a plastic bag, no doubt, or the remains of some child's bucket and spade. But when she bent to retrieve it, it was a bright red scarf with a picture of an Irish Setter in the middle of it. She clutched it to herself, suddenly feeling dizzy. It was such a familiar scarf that she almost knew the actual look on the setter's face and felt for the label she'd always told Charlie to cut off.

'It looks silly hanging off,' she'd said.

'But it's a designer label. I need to keep it on so everyone knows I know someone rich enough to buy me a designer scarf. And he's just like my lovely Jasper was.'

Clutching the soggy scarf close to her face, Emma felt as if she could drag out the very scent of her friend. It was real, tangible proof that Charlie had been here, proof that she had not died on her way down to Cornwall after all.

# CHAPTER 5

What is it?' Sam asked as he walked across to where Emma stood, looking pale and trembling. 'What have you found?'

But Emma couldn't answer. Tears of relief streamed down her face. 'It's Charlie's favourite scarf,' she managed to say between sobs. 'So . . . so she really did get here.'

'OK,' he said cautiously. 'But how do you know this is her scarf? There must be a hundred like it.'

'I know it's hers. The picture is like Jasper, her lovely dog she used to have. And the label, see how it's almost falling off? I used to tease her about it and . . . and . . . oh, I know this was hers. She always wore it.'

'OK, so it looks possible, but where can she be now? Why isn't she answering your calls?'

'But it's clear evidence, isn't it? Evidence that she did come here. Along with my other suspicions, doesn't it mean you need to investigate it further?'

'I just don't know. It does seem more compelling but the chief seems to think there's no doubt. I mean, who was the person in the car if it wasn't Charlie? So, what do you think is the scenario? Explain it, if you can.'

'Maybe Charlie did arrive early last Saturday. Maybe she parked her car at the top in that sort of parking area—she wouldn't know about the Crelly's farm track—and she walked down to the cottage, had a quick look, went back to the garage, probably bought some milk and stuff and saw the postcard. She wrote the card and posted it. There's a post box near the farm so she might have put it in there. That would explain why it hadn't been collected until Monday. Then she went down to look at the beach and found the cave. She'd have been interested in that. Then she somehow dropped her scarf and went back to collect her stuff from the car. Only by then, the car had been stolen and driven off. Something happened and it was set on fire, by accident or design, and someone was trapped inside. I don't know exactly where or when it was found.'

'In a little side road off the A30. South of Hayle,' Sam said.

'So if she was on her way down here, why would she have turned off the main road?'

'You've thought it all out, certainly. But I can still see a few flaws. When she saw the state of the cottage, would she have simply left it and gone to the beach? I mean, you know yourself what you thought of the place and you immediately went to buy some things. And if she'd bought milk or anything else, it would have still been here when you arrived.'

'Don't be so picky. I'm working on the plot as I go. I swear this climb is twice as steep as it was yesterday.'

'Nearly at the top. Do you want a hand?'

'Tempting but I'm OK.'

They flopped down on the grassy bank when they reached the top. It was hot and they both sat quietly for a while until Emma remembered the bottle of water and passed it to him.

'You mean to say, you had this with you all the time?'

'Sorry, I forgot. My mind can only cope with one thing at a time.' She smiled at him, her whole body and soul seemingly cheered by her latest discovery. Now it was only matter of finding out what had actually happened to her friend.

Sam watched her face as he handed the bottle back. She wiped the neck of it and took a long swig.

'You look quite different now. As if a load has been lifted off you. You're really very pretty when you don't frown.'

'Are you flirting with me?'

'Not really, just making an observation.'

'You're not so bad yourself.'

Sam was nice looking in an ordinary sort of way; fair hair, blue eyes and a lovely smile. He was fit and kept himself in trim with his daily runs. Best of all, he was an ally and Emma felt sure he would support her now in her quest to find her friend.

He smiled and touched her hand. 'We need

to keep things separate, you know. I'll do what I can to help you but if we're seeing each other outside work, I don't want to be doing anything unofficially.'

'Seeing each other? How do you mean?'

'Well, yes . . . like today. I'm not suggesting there's more to it but this is my day off and not official police business.'

'But you have to help me track down Charlie. You have to see that I was right, in view of the new evidence,' she added.

He forced a smiled. 'Maybe I should give Mum a call. Let her know we're on our way.'

'If you're sure it won't embarrass you?'

'Don't be silly. Friends?' Sam smiled at her and stood up, dialling a number on his mobile as he did so.

Emma half listened but her mind was fully occupied with thoughts of Charlie. She knew her logic was flawed, but something must have happened to Charlie. If her scenario was correct and the car had been stolen, then she must have been taken somewhere. Or had an accident. Suppose she had fallen over the cliff and her body washed out to sea? That was almost as bad as the car crash.

Emma's mood swung again and her happiness at finding the scarf was immediately quashed. Sam came back to her.

'Ready to go? Mum's thrilled. Don't be put off by her though. I don't take many girls home so she might make assumptions and think there's something between us, so don't mind her.'

'I know the feeling. Any male in tow and my mother was planning the wedding hat . . .' Emma broke off and unexpected tears pressed behind her eyes. She blinked them away and swallowed to regain control. 'Sorry. Take no notice.'

'You can tell me if you like.'

She shook her head. 'Things best forgotten. Now, do you want to walk or go in the car? How far is it anyway?'

'It's probably a couple of miles. I suggest the car, if you don't mind. You must be pretty tired after that climb. I'm used to these paths but you're not.'

'The car it is. Just give me a minute to change my shoes.'

Emma unlocked the door and the piece of paper dropped out. It had been undisturbed. She bent to pick it up.

'What's that about?' asked Sam.

'I think someone's been coming in and moving my things. I thought this would show me if anyone had been in today.'

'You shouldn't have to put up with that,' Sam said seriously. 'Who do you think it is?'

'I assume it's Rob Grenville. I think he must still have a key.'

'Have you asked him?'

'Well no. I haven't seen him again. Not since the first morning when he wouldn't even give me a cup of coffee.'

'You want me to go and see him?'

'Officially or unofficially?'

'I could go in uniform. Make it a formal complaint.'

'No, that might get unpleasant. It's OK. Leave it. I'll keep putting my paper in the door so at least I'll know.'

'You ought to have a security camera.'

'Oh, like I'm going to lay out money for something like that here?' Emma laughed.

'I'll see if I can borrow one for you. These motion sensor things that record for a few minutes when there's movement. We can put it inside the door so we can see if anyone comes in.'

'Sounds amazing. Modern technology, eh?'

They climbed through the fence and got into the overheated car and Emma drove carefully across the field.

'Oh good,' she said. 'You can open and close the gates so I won't get surrounded by cows.'

'Heifers aren't they?'

'Still cows to me. What's a heifer anyway?'

'A young female before it's had a calf.'

'They're pretty big for young creatures.'

'Quite a townie, aren't you?' Sam laughed.

'Just go and open the gate, Braveheart,' Emma laughed too.

* * *

When they arrived at Sam's house, his mother came rushing out to greet them.

'I'm so pleased to meet you. Emma, isn't it?'

The tiny, almost bird like woman held out a hand. Her blue eyes peered out of a face wrinkled prematurely from too much exposure to the sun. It was clear to see where Sam got his colouring and her eyes looked very much like his.

'Of course. Pleased to meet you Mrs Henley.'

'Oh please call me Joan. I gather you're here on holiday?'

'It was supposed to be a holiday but it's all gone pear-shaped. I expect Sam's told you the gist of it.'

'Oh no, dear, he never talks about his work. I get quite frustrated at times when he's so secretive, especially when he knows stuff that would interest me.'

'Mum, you know it's more than my job's worth.'

'So tell me something about yourself,' Joan said to Emma as they sat down at a table loaded with enough food to feed a small army, just as Sam had warned her.

'There's not a great deal to tell . . . unless I can talk about my particular problem?' she asked Sam, eyebrows raised.

'I suppose it can't hurt. It's up to you. I won't comment though,' Sam replied.

'To start at the beginning. It seems that the old lady who lived at Gull Cottage . . .' she began.

'Martha,' Joan interrupted. 'Help yourself to vegetables.'

'Thank you . . . yes, Martha was a distant relative of my friend Charlie, Charlotte Danvers. Unexpectedly, she left the cottage to Charlie, who decided to come down for a holiday and invited me to come along.'

'Fancy Martha having relatives. After all this time and we never knew it. She was quite eccentric, you know.'

'So I gather.'

'She used to walk miles along the cliff paths regularly, right up to her demise. She used to call in for a cuppa when she was passing. My husband, God rest his soul, used to get quite wearied by her when she stayed chatting for hours, especially during the summer evenings. He came home expecting his tea and there was Martha, gossiping nineteen to the dozen.'

'I thought you wanted to hear about Emma?' Sam said, smiling. This was typical of his mother. Asked a question and never listened, even if someone was willing to answer her.

'It's alright,' Emma replied. 'I want to hear about Martha. How did she cope with living so frugally? I mean there's nothing much at the cottage, it's all very basic.'

'She did fine by herself alright. Had a little

generator in that shed in the garden to run the basics, a fridge and so on, and a chemical toilet in the back scullery, so it wasn't too bad. She had some nice furniture too. We used to laugh, my late husband and me. What on earth did she want with fine antiques when she'd got so little in the way of amenities? She could easily have had electricity put in. The Crelly's have it and she could have had it joined on from them. We used to reckon she made her extra money from helping the smugglers.'

Mrs Henley waved an open hand at the serving dishes. 'Come on now, eat up. There's plenty more.'

Sam had been eating steadily and passed his plate over for a second helping. His mother scarcely ate anything, but she had been talking none stop.

'I wonder what happened to the furniture? There's next to nothing there now.'

'Really? I haven't been along she since she passed away. I'd have thought the contents were left along with the cottage.'

'Maybe I should ask the solicitor. I suppose you don't know which one she used, do you?'

'Oh yes, dear. Taylor and Murchison in Penzance. In the high street they are. You think they might tell you?'

'I doubt it, but it might answer some questions.'

'So now, where's this 'ere friend of yours? I hope you didn't leave her behind, our Sam.'

'Course not. That's part of the mystery. Charlie never arrived here. We think she'd been in a road accident on the way down.'

'Oh, not that dreadful one in the paper? Oh, you poor dear! What a terrible thing to happen. You weren't with her then?'

'No. I couldn't come down 'till last week. But I really don't believe it was her.'

Emma told Joan about the postcard, the phone call and finally the scarf they'd found. 'So you see, she wasn't in the car at all. I think it'd been stolen and then set on fire.'

'But Sam's helping investigate, I s'ppose?'

'Sort of. He's been very kind, even though he has doubts about my stories. I appreciated him coming along to check up on me. It's a pretty spooky place, Gull Cottage.'

'Especially for a townie,' Sam teased.

'For anyone who isn't used to it, what with all those creaks and groans,' Emma corrected.

'And no doubt you've met the delightful Rob Grenville?'

'I would hardly call him delightful. He scared me a bit.'

'He's usually up to no good. Probably worried you'd be poking your nose into his affairs,' Joan said.

'He had the keys to the cottage but it was unlocked when I arrived. He was a bit put out to say the least when I turned up.'

'I wonder . . .' Joan began, but she refused to say any more after a warning glance from

76

her son.

'Could he . . . do you think he might have had something to do with Charlie's disappearance?' Emma said, wide-eyed.

'I'd doubt it. He usually works for other people. He hasn't got the brains to think of too many things for himself.'

'You're gossiping again, Mum,' Sam chided. 'You shouldn't give our guest the wrong ideas about the place.'

'Well, alright, but you must admit, it's a bit suspicious that the place has been stripped of everything and he had the keys. I did hear there was someone squatting, after Martha passed on, God rest her soul.'

'Maybe they took everything then,' Emma suggested. 'Perhaps. We'll never know.'

'So who is it that Rob works for?' Emma asked.

'Anyone who'll employ him,' Joan told her. 'He does some labouring for the bulb growers along the coast . . . the fish place, too, and there's a big produce processing company outside Penzance. They contract the vegetable packing with local farmers. I'm not sure quite what he does but he seems to be involved with them in some way.'

Emma turned to Sam. 'Is this why you think he might have something to do with bringing in immigrants?'

'It's no more than a suspicion,' Sam replied. 'But enough of all this talk. Mum, tell me

77

you've made some pudding?'

'Course I have. I know better than to serve Sunday lunch to you without a pudding. Can you cook Emma?'

'A bit. Not up to your standard, though. That was wonderful. Best Sunday lunch I've had in years. I'll help you clear up.'

'Don't you dare. You sit right there, you're a guest. Sam will help.' She turned to her son and told him, 'Bring the leftover meat and veg. I'll make something out of them for tomorrow.'

Awkwardly, Emma sat at the table while her hosts busied themselves in the kitchen. Joan came back carrying possibly the largest pie Emma had ever seen outside a restaurant.

'I hope you like plums. These are from our tree. First of the season. You timed it just right.'

'How lovely. Not too huge a piece, thank you. I'm full of the lovely first course.'

'Nonsense dear. You need building up after your terrible shock. Just leave what you don't want.' A vast piece of pie was placed before her. Sam gave her a warning glance which seemed to say, *you'd better not leave any.*

After dinner they sat out in the pretty garden for coffee.

'I'm glad I drove. I doubt I could even walk down the path let alone all the way back to the cottage,' Emma said, replete.

'So what are your plans? Are you going to

stay on at the cottage or are you going back home?' Joan Henley asked.

'I plan to stay on for a while. I have to try to find out what happened to Charlie. I'll go and see the solicitors tomorrow and see if it's all right if I stay on. If I can't stay at the cottage, I suppose I'll have to find a B&B or something.

Joan glanced at Sam and raised her eyebrows questioningly.

He nodded. 'You could always come and stay here. We've plenty of room. In a way, I'd be offering it for Martha's sake.'

'That's incredibly kind, thank you. But is that alright with you Sam? It's not mixing work and social life too much?'

'I guess not. They needn't know at the station, anyway.'

'I'll have to come in and present my latest evidence . . .'

'I'll make sure you see the sergeant and the woman officer you saw the other day, though I'm not sure they'll believe you or agree to take further action.'

'Then I'll have to do it myself, won't I?'

'Look, I don't want to put a dampener on anything but you should prepare yourself for the worst. It may be that Charlie did come here as you think, and I admit it does seem possible, but she must have gone somewhere. It could be that she fell over the cliffs or was hurt in some way, maybe even drowned.'

'No way, Charlie was a terrific swimmer. If

she went into the sea at all, she would have been able to swim back.'

Emma was vehement in her denials. Hope for Charlie's survival was not being taken away from her again.

'OK, don't get upset. But if she fell, hit her head or something, she may not have been able to swim.'

'Stop it, Sam,' insisted his mother. 'Let Emma keep her hopes alive.'

'I don't want her to build them up too high. That's all.'

'You must be able to help her look for her friend, our Sam.'

'There's only so much I can do. There's nothing back from forensics about the burnt-out car, not as far as I know.'

'The officer I saw yesterday said the car was still with those people. Surely there's something suspicious about it? I mean, isn't a body in a car enough to cause an enquiry?'

'They think they're certain about who it is. I expect they'll be checking it out to make sure it was an accident but resources are always getting reduced. It has to be something highly suspicious. You wouldn't believe the number of car wrecks there are. They nick them, set them on fire and shove them over a remote cliff somewhere. We don't always know if there was even a body in them. If we can't get down to them, the sea rots them away to nothing.'

'That's terrible. But this one wasn't even shoved over a cliff. Just in a side road, you said.'

'I know, it's the way things are, I'm afraid.'

'So will they try to contact Charlie's parents?'

'They'll have to get into her home to find their address. Unless you know someone who knows where they live?'

'Sorry, no, but they have Charlie's address from the car's records, I assume?'

'Oh yes. They'll get the local police to go round. Do you know if anyone has a key?' Sam asked.

'Neighbours do, I expect.'

'Did she have a boyfriend?'

'No-one special. She's always been a bit of a party girl . . .' Emma paused. 'Shouldn't you be writing all this down?'

'Not really. I assume you've told the detectives all this already. I'm just getting a bit of a picture for myself.'

'I suppose I'd better go back to the cottage. It's been lovely. Thank you so much Mrs Henley—Joan,' Emma said.

'I meant what I said about you coming to stay here if you need to. You'd be very welcome.'

'Thank you again. And thank you Sam for your company—and for inviting me for lunch.'

*　　　*　　　*

Emma drove back feeling a mixture of being happier but still feeling a bit sad and confused. She stopped at the garage to see if Colin was there but he was still absent, so she'd have to call round one evening when he got back from whatever he did during the day. Now she had positive proof that Charlie had been to Bodilly Cove, she felt slightly less concerned about what he might have to say.

Driving down the now familiar track across the fields, Emma waved to Mrs Crelly as she passed the farm. The woman came over to the gate and waved her down.

'You managing alright down there?' she asked.

'Not bad, thank you. It's a great help using your field track.'

'Have you heard any more about the accident? I saw the report in the local paper.'

'Not a lot but the good news is that Charlie definitely did come here on the Saturday. I found her scarf in the cave down there and I'm sure she still has her phone. So you see, it couldn't have been her in the car.'

'Well I never. So who was it?'

'I don't know, but I'm going to the police station tomorrow.'

'Are you eating properly?' she asked suddenly.

'Oh yes. I've just been for Sunday lunch with Mrs Henley and Sam. I doubt I shall need to eat again for several days!'

'She's a lovely cook. So sad she lost her husband so young, but Sam came back to be with her so she's more fortunate than many I could name. Well, I mustn't keep you. I hope you find your friend in the end. Pop in for a cuppa tomorrow when you get back from the police station and tell me the latest news.'

'Thank you, Mrs Crelly, I will.'

Emma drove down the field and felt comforted by the renewed acts of kindness from people. She parked behind the hedge and climbed through, where she could see several groups of people walking below her, along the popular coastal path. She pushed open the sagging gate and went to unlock the door.

The key didn't turn and she gave it a push. It was open and her scrap of paper was lying on the floor. Clearly someone had been in and left the door unlocked. Emma was certain she'd locked it. Besides, Sam would have noticed if she hadn't secured it properly.

Anxiously, she pushed it open and went in cautiously. She gripped her bag tightly in her fist, ready to use it as a weapon if necessary. Hadn't Anthony always teased her that it weighed as much as if she had several bricks in it?

The kitchen looked pretty much as she had left it and so did the lounge. Cautiously, she went upstairs and looked in the bedrooms. Nobody was there and she relaxed.

Apart from being slightly rumpled, her sleeping bag was still in place and the bundle of sweaters she was using as a pillow looked just the same. It may have been exactly as she left it but she did feel as if it might have been moved. She shivered. It was horrid to think of anyone touching her things. Maybe she should take up the Henley's offer, but somehow, she felt she needed to stay here, just in case Charlie returned.

Still feeling very full, Emma sat in the garden to try to relax. She didn't want to worry Sam by telling him about the intruder, especially as there was little he could do about it. Lifting the book she'd bought, she tried to read it, but the words danced in front of her eyes as she turned several pages but took in none of it. What she needed to do was to make notes of everything that had happened and maybe even speculate on possible scenarios. She would make a proper 'to do' list. She took out the little notebook she kept in her bag and began to write. She was determined to discover what had happened to Charlie.

# CHAPTER 6

With Charlie's scarf, now dry but still smelling slightly salty, beside her on her pillow Emma fell asleep. Occasionally she stirred and felt for the comfort of the scarf as if it was somehow bringing Charlie closer.

She woke suddenly as dawn was just beginning to lighten the sky. She heard something that had disturbed her and crept out of bed, peering through the small, grubby window, but she could see nothing. She went to the other bedroom and looked out of the other side of the house, where she could see several people moving along the path, close to the hedge. They stopped outside the cottage.

Emma froze, hardly daring to breathe in case she made a sound, as she drew back from the window and pulled on her fleece. She started to creep down the stairs. There was a loud bang at the door and she stood still, terrified they might have heard her moving. She heard the door knob rattle and her heart began to pound almost out of control. She crept back upstairs to grab her phone, searching for Sam's number, ready to dial if they managed to open the door.

The door rattled again and someone called out, 'Come on. Open up. What the hell are you doing?' It was a foreign accent.

Another bang and that was it; she dialled Sam's number.

'Come on, answer,' she said whispered urgently.

'Emma? What's up?' he answered sleepily.

'There's someone trying to get in. Several people outside. Banging on the door. They're asking to be let in.'

'Where are you?'

'Upstairs. Sam, I'm scared. I don't know who it is.'

'Stay there. I'll be there as soon as I can. I'll call the station and get some back-up once I'm on my way. Don't answer them and don't open the door.'

Sam's phone went off and Emma stood still, quaking with terror. Who on earth could it be at this hour of the morning?

She stood against the wall and tried to peer out through the side without being seen. Whoever it was had gone quiet, but she could see three people standing in the garden, talking in a huddled group. They looked like females but it was difficult to tell; they had scarves over their heads, leaving only the middle part of their faces exposed. They had long coats on, looking quite old fashioned, and each one was carrying a small bundle of something indefinable.

There was one last bang at the door and they all turned and walked away down the lane and she saw them continue down onto the coastal path, walking slowly in the direction of Rob Grenville's cottage. She felt concerned that she had called Sam, as now there was nothing here for him to see. She knew she was guilty of panicking but anyone would have to agree it was scary and was certainly not something normal to be happening.

Emma moved the chair from its customary place propped against the door and turned the key in the lock. Slowly, she opened the door and peered out, as if she was half expecting to see someone still waiting outside. She heard the sound of a motor bike coming along the coastal path and ducked inside again, ready to slam the door shut if necessary. As she watched through the window and a helmeted figure pushed open the gate and unhooked the helmet and she sighed with relief when she saw it was Sam. As he came in through the door she flung her arms round him.

'Hey, it's alright,' he murmured, stroking her hair. 'I'm here. You're safe now.'

'Sorry,' she said as she detached herself. 'I was so frightened. Someone had been in here yesterday again. They even left the door unlocked.'

'You should have called me right away.'

'It was alright. Nothing had been touched.'

'But if someone has a key, you're not safe at night.'

'I shove that big old chair against the door. But this morning, they only banged at the door and tried to turn the knob to open it. The lock held, but I was so scared. I wasn't sure what would have happened if they'd actually got in.'

'So tell me exactly what happened.'

With her hands still trembling slightly, Emma filled her little saucepan to make some coffee while she recounted the story.

'I was woken by some sort of noise. I went to look out of the window and then the window in the other room. I could see shadowy shapes in the garden. There were at least three of them. Then someone was banging at the door but the three women—I think they were women—stood back.'

'What did they look like?'

'I couldn't see much. It was still fairly dark and they were in the shadows, and they had sort of head scarves on, wrapped round so you could only see the middle of their faces. And long dark coloured coats, a bit old fashioned looking.'

'Where did they go?'

'Back to the coastal path, towards Rob's cottage.'

'Did you hear any vehicles? Boats, engines or anything?'

'Well, no. I didn't really listen, though. Oh yes, the man with them who was calling out, he had a foreign accent. I was inside and stayed upstairs 'till they'd gone.' She sighed with renewed relief. 'I didn't realise you had a motorbike . . .'

'It's only a moped really but it gets me along the path quicker than trying to drive here, even using the Crelly's track. I'll see if any of the lads are near yet, then we'll go and tackle Rob. We can take a look round and see if he's got any unusual visitors.'

'Who do you think they are?'

'Possibly some of the illegals we mentioned before.'

'But why would they come here?'

'Who knows? Maybe they could have been using this place after Martha died, or possibly even before. Perhaps she was involved in some way.'

'Goodness. What have I walked into?' The water was boiling. 'Do you want some coffee?'

'Better not. I should go and meet up with the others. They must be walking down the lane.'

'Be careful, Sam,' Emma said. 'You never know who they are. It could be dangerous.'

'Don't worry, but thanks for the concern. Shut your door again and make some coffee for yourself and I'll try to come back later and let you know if I find out anything.'

Emma watched as he got back on his little moped and drove carefully along the narrow path. It was only just wide enough. She would never have dared risk driving so near to the edge but he was obviously used to it and was soon out of sight.

She made herself some coffee and watched

through the window to see if anyone else was coming along. As the sun rose, the room was becoming warmer and she opened a window to let in some air. It was a long wait for something to happen. What a start to the week!

As eight o'clock approached, Emma had calmed down and her pulse had returned to something like normal. It seemed unlikely that Sam would come back as he was probably due at work soon, so she washed herself at the sink, as had become usual the last few days and she no longer cringed at the cold water. All the same, she longed for a proper shower and proper facilities again. She would never again complain about the lack of hot water when she returned home and nor would she mind about cleaning the bathroom.

So many things she took for granted and it was sad to think of Martha living her entire life in these conditions, especially if she'd had money enough to make improvements.

Once she had dressed and made more coffee, Emma sat at the table and looked over her 'to do' list. At the top she had written *Police,* and under the heading she had listed her reasons for believing it wasn't Charlie in the burnt out car:

*Postcard*
*Phone voice*
*mail*
*Charlie's scarf*

To Emma, it seemed pretty compelling and somehow, she needed to convince the detective of just that—they must investigate it now, surely?

Second on her list was *Visit Solicitors*. She was less certain she would be able to gain any information from them but it was worth a try. They might at least be able to tell her if the cottage had been left to Charlie with the contents included. If not, then where had the contents been sent? If they were left with the cottage, then someone needed to investigate a potential theft. Not that it was really her business but it needed to be raised.

Her final 'to do' was a visit to the newspaper office to see if there was a report of Martha's death. Were there any suspicious circumstances or were they completely satisfied with the theory of an accident? Perhaps she might also ask Sam or the other officers.

Emma had also written a report of what she felt might have happened that fateful Saturday. It was pure speculation and left a large number of unanswered questions, the most challenging one being what had actually happened to Charlie? If she wasn't in the car, where was she now and why had nobody seen anything of her for over a week?

Clearly, strange things were going on in this seemingly quiet cove in Cornwall. She glanced at her watch, wondering what time the police station would be open.

Her phone rang and Sam's name showed up on the screen.

'Hi Sam. How's it going?'

'Nothing to report, I'm afraid. We've searched Rob's place thoroughly. He wasn't too pleased of course but there's no sign of anyone there. He protested that we were invading his privacy and all that, but it didn't stop us. I don't really understand where your mysterious group of people disappeared to. We've been further along the cliff path and back up the lane towards the main road but still no sign of anyone.'

'Do you think someone came to pick them up?'

'We don't know. Perhaps. I'm sorry I haven't come back to see you but it's time I was at work and I still have to go home and change.'

'I'm coming into the station anyway so I'll see you later.'

'They'll want a statement from you about this morning too.'

'I can't say much.'

'No, but your call resulted in a call out. They'll need to put it in the report. It's all about filling in forms these days.'

'Tell me about it. And computers were supposed to stop the paper mountains. I mustn't keep you. Thanks for everything.'

'See you later.'

Emma wandered round the unkempt garden, tugging the occasional weed out. She felt anxious, frustrated and was jumpy with every sound she heard. She kept hearing noises even when they weren't there and wondered how much longer she could bear to stay here.

The idea of Sam's mother providing delicious meals and being company were almost too tempting but she knew that really, she needed to stay here. This cottage must have some clues hidden away, something to indicate what could have happened to Charlie—and possibly even to Martha.

Suddenly, Emma jumped at the creak of the gate. This time it was real and the angry figure of Rob Grenville stood menacingly blocking her way along the path back to the cottage.

She took a deep breath to steady her nerves and stood very still. 'Mr Grenville,' she began, but her mouth was dry and a squeak came out instead of the firm voice she had intended.

'You wants to get yourself back to where you'm come from. Stop meddlin' with stuff as you know nowt about. Set the cops on to me this mornin' din't ya? Not good. Not good for you neither. Tek my advice and get gone.'

'I'm sorry but I didn't set the cops on you, as you put it. I was disturbed at dawn by someone banging on my door. I expect, as yours is the next house along the path, they called on you to see if you'd heard or seen anything.'

'How'd you know that? 'Specially if you didn't send them.'

'You just told me they'd been to yours. That seems a likely reason. Now, if you'll excuse me, I have things to do.'

'Mark my words. You needs to get gone. Get right away from here and stop meddlin' in stuff as you has no business with.'

'My friend is missing; that makes it my business.'

'Her's burnt up. Burnt to a crisp,' he said his eyes gleaming with some sort of triumph. 'So you might as well get gone.'

'I thought you said she'd never arrived here?'

'She din't. Never showed. Got 'erself burnt to a crisp instead,' he repeated with relish.

'But I know she did arrive. I have proof.'

The man stared and an expression of anger came over him as he moved menacingly towards her. She shrank back.

'You can't 'ave. She never came, I tells you.' He raised his fist and Emma moved back even further. Pulling her phone out of her pocket she lifted it to dial Sam's number.

'What you doin'? Gimme that contraption.'

'Get away from me!'

Emma pressed the re-dial button and prayed that Sam was in a position to answer or at least listen.

'Alright,' she said and shoved it back in her pocket, careful not switch it off.

'You need to take care. If you stay round 'ere, you could meet a fate like . . .' he paused. 'You could find yoursen' in the sort of trouble as you wouldn't like.'

'What were you going to say? Like my friend? Or like poor old Martha?'

'What d'you know about that?'

'Martha? That she was fit and healthy just before she died. I reckon it would bear some more investigation.'

'You's a trouble maker. Just watch out.'

'And what do you know about the furniture that should have been here? Martha had some good pieces, so I hear.'

'You'm hearin' wrong then. None o' your business. Tek my advice and get gone.'

He turned and walked away, then stopped and shook his fist at her, drawing his hand across his throat in a threatening way.

Emma gave a shudder as she took her phone out of her pocket but it had gone dead. The battery had finally given out.

Mrs Crelly had offered to recharge it for her. Maybe she could drop it off on her way out. It was important, vital even, for her to have her phone, which was her only contact with the world outside Bodilly Cove. Besides, without it, she had no way of summoning help if she needed it. Amazing how much one came to rely on being connected with the world.

She locked up the cottage, carefully inserting her piece of paper in the crack and set off up the farm track. She stopped at the farm house and knocked on the back door and heard a dog bark somewhere inside but nobody came to answer her. Knocking again, she looked across the yard into one of the barns and walked over there, calling out as she went in.

It seemed to be filled with farm machinery and piles of what looked like boxes, covered with tarpaulins and old sheets, but there was nobody around. She called out again and walked towards what she assumed was the milking parlour but there was still no response. Perhaps they were already out working the fields. One good idea done with. She'd have to hope Sam would charge the phone for her, either at his home or even at the police station. She put the phone and charger back into her bag and set off up the lane. At least Sam should be at work by now.

She drove into Penzance, trying a car park further into the town, to save her the long walk, then went into the police station and asked if Sam was on duty.

'Afraid he's gone out on a call. He got a phone call and went rushing off like a bat out of hell.'

'Oh dear, I expect that was me. I dialled his number and the battery must have gone flat before I could speak.'

'Did you have a problem at the time?'

'Well, yes. I was being threatened and I called his number. I shoved my phone into my pocket and hoped he would be able to hear what was happening. He must have rushed to my place and I must have passed him on the way.'

'Can I help?'

'I need to see the detective I saw the other day, if possible.'

'And your name?'

'Emma Peterson.'

'Can you say what it's in connection with?'

'Long story. It was my friend and she's missing but it wasn't her in the car wreck, like everyone seems to think. I've got some more proof, you see.'

'I'll try and find someone for you to speak to. Take a seat.'

'I don't suppose I could put my phone on to charge somewhere?' Emma asked. 'I know it's a bit of a cheek but I don't have electricity where I'm staying. And since I'm being threatened and it's my only means of communicating...'

'Oh, go on then. I expect you were hoping Sam would do it.'

'Well, yes. Can you call him and tell him I got here safely?'

'Anything else, madam?' Emma smiled at him and raised her eyebrows and he went on, 'Are you and Sam, well . . . are you going out or something?'

'Oh no, nothing like that. He lives quite near where I'm staying and has been helping me, that's all.'

'Give me your phone and the charger, then and I'll plug it in over there for you.'

'Thank you very much. Very kind of you.'

Emma went and sat down and after a few minutes, the sergeant she had seen on Friday came to take her through.

'What can I do for you?' he asked.

'A couple of more things have happened,' Emma said. 'Things that make me even more convinced that it wasn't my friend, Charlie who was in the car.'

He gave a slightly pitying smile. 'You'd better tell me then.' He took out the folder with her statement and indicated that she should sit opposite him. 'So what have you learned?'

'There's the postcard I let you have on Friday. There's only one shop selling them and they're old stock. Nobody else has bought them in months. That was the first thing. Secondly, I've found a scarf belonging to Charlie. I recognised it immediately. It was one of her favourites.'

'And where exactly did you find it?'

'There's a huge cave on the beach just below the cottage. It was in there, quite near the back.'

'And why were you looking in the cave?'

'This probably sounds silly but people have been telling me about some sort of old passage that leads from the cottage down to the cave. A relic of smuggling days, they say.'

'And this convinces you, how?'

'Charlie wore this scarf all the time, it was sort of her lucky mascot. Here it is. The picture is like the dog she used to have. Jasper, an Irish Setter.' She took it out of her bag and handed it to the man, who glanced at it briefly.

'There must be dozens of these around. What makes you think it belongs to your friend? And how does this prove she wasn't in the car?'

'It is hers. I know it. Look—the label's hanging off. I kept telling her to cut it off, but she wouldn't. It was a bit of a joke between us—a designer label—but it proves she went to the cottage in the first place, despite what everyone thinks.'

'And why do you think she would have gone down to the beach before moving her things into the cottage? From what you say, it's pretty basic in there. Would she have really gone for a paddle in the sea, rather than settling in?'

'I don't know,' Emma said hopelessly. 'Maybe she was tired after the long drive and wanted a walk.'

'Maybe, but what was to stop her driving out again? The accident was during the evening so perhaps she went out to meet someone. Or to get a meal?'

'But why would she drive so far in that direction?'

'Was there something else?' He was closing his folder.

'Well yes. I called her mobile number. I've been calling it quite regularly and it's usually been dead. But when I dialled it on Saturday, I got her voice mail. I came into the station to tell the desk officer but when he tried it, it was dead again.'

'If it hasn't happened again, I'd be certain it was a freak random incident. Now, if that's it, I must say goodbye to you. I'll be in contact if anything develops.'

'But you can't just ignore me. What about DNA samples? And how do you know the fire was an accident? Doesn't there have to be an investigation?'

'Excuse me. I'll go and check to see if there's any report from forensics yet.'

'Thank you. I'll wait here, shall I?'

'Well, yes, alright. I'll be back in a minute.'

As it turned out, it was more like fifteen minutes. Emma sat biting her nails. Not only was she feeling increasingly frustrated, she was becoming angry. Surely what she had given them was enough to investigate further?

At last, Sergeant Davies returned, still carrying what she thought of as her file.

'Preliminary investigations suggest the car was deliberately set on fire. The driver's seat had been liberally doused in petrol, including the driver herself. The whole car was then torched and burned, particularly the front end and interior. The boot which must have held the travel bag we showed you, collapsed under the heat and the scorched remains of the bag fell out.'

'That's terrible! Do you think the driver was dead before being covered in petrol?' She shuddered at the thought of someone doing this dreadful act so callously, so deliberately.

'I would think so. Or at least unconscious, perhaps. Nobody could have survived such a concentration of heat.'

'So, is getting any DNA even possible? The big questions are who it was and if it wasn't Charlie, where can she be now?'

'As you say, big questions indeed. It does throw a different light on matters, now that we know it was a deliberate act of arson. They are looking into the DNA sampling and also the jaw. Dental records might still be possible to check. You'll have to leave matters with us now, Miss Peterson. We'll be in touch if we hear any news. In the meantime, I suggest you consider returning to your own home. You'll be under less stress if you do, I'm sure. Familiar things around you. Routine.'

'I can't possibly leave without knowing the truth. Or at least coming somewhere near knowing the truth. Do you know if you've made any progress on finding out about the people knocking on my door at dawn today?'

'Sorry. I don't know anything about that.'

'Sam Henley was dealing with it.'

'I haven't seen him today. One of the others must be dealing with it. Now, if you'll excuse me, I must get on.'

Unwillingly, Emma got up and followed him to the door.

'I'm sorry but we are handing it over to the CID officers now. They'll probably want to speak to you once they've familiarised themselves with the details. We have your phone number on record so we'll call you later.'

'My battery's flat and I don't have power where I'm staying. The desk officer is charging it for me. Sorry if that's wrong but I was desperate and begged him. I hope he won't be in trouble.'

'I think we can possibly stand the cost of a phone battery charge,' he said with the first hint of a smile she'd seen.

'Thank you. And thanks for your time.'

'No problem. Sorry not to have been of more help. And take my advice. Go back home.'

She didn't reply and left with a faint smile.

'Any luck?' asked the desk sergeant.

'Not really. Only that it was a deliberate fire, not an accident. How's my phone doing?'

'Not there yet. Do you want to wait?'

'I think I'd better. Have you heard from Sam yet?'

'On his way back. Take a seat. He won't be long.'

Emma sat impatiently watching people come and go. People who had lost pets. People claiming to have been robbed. They were dealt with efficiently after forms were filled in and they left being told they would be notified if there was any information. How many of them would actually hear again, she wondered? At last Sam arrived.

'Are you alright? I heard Rob Grenville shouting at you over your phone. Then the phone went off and I rushed out.'

'I'm sorry. He wanted me to hand the phone over so I shoved it in my pocket. The battery went flat but he left soon after that. I was pretty scared at the time, but I suspect my nerves are shattered anyway after this morning and everything else.'

'You really should move out of there. It isn't safe for you to be there on your own and it's so remote, nobody can get to you quickly in an emergency.'

'Thank you but I have to stick it out. If Charlie comes back, that's where she'll look for me.'

'Oh, Emma . . . you have to face up to the possibility that she won't come back.'

'But don't you see? The car was fired deliberately. They'll start to take it more seriously now, surely? The driver was probably murdered before they burnt it to get rid of the body. They'll have to try to identify the body won't they?'

'Yes, but from what I hear, there's not much left . . .'

'It isn't Charlie. I know it isn't Charlie,' she hissed through teeth clenched to stop herself from crying.

# CHAPTER 7

With little hope of them giving her any information, Emma walked along the main street looking for the solicitors who had dealt with Martha's estate. Taylor and Murchison shouldn't be too difficult to find. She just hoped someone would agree to speak to her.

She spotted the office on the other side of the road and crossed. There were steep steps on the other side, making it a difficult street to cross, especially for some of the mothers with prams and push chairs and elderly folk. She pushed open the door and spoke to the receptionist. When she explained the situation, the young woman looked dubious.

'I'm not sure if there's anyone free who might be able to help you,' she said haughtily.

An elderly man came through from the back and spoke to the woman without noticing Emma.

'Miss Wilkes, could you call this number for

me? Ask them if they've . . .' he broke off. 'Oh, I do beg your pardon. I didn't see you there, madam.'

'Actually Mr Brown, would you have a moment to talk to Miss . . . sorry, I didn't catch your name.'

'Peterson. Emma Peterson.'

'How can I help?' he asked.

'I wanted to ask if you could give me some information about the estate of Martha—oh my goodness, I don't even know her second name. My very close friend Charlotte Danvers recently inherited Martha's cottage at Bodilly Cove.'

'Yes, I know the case. I dealt with the probate myself. But I'm not sure how I can be of help?'

'Charlie—Charlotte—has disappeared. The police are investigating. At least, I'm hoping they are. They thought she was killed in a car accident last week but I'm certain it wasn't her. The thing is, I was coming to stay with Charlie and when I arrived, I found the cottage empty . . . well, practically empty and no sign of Charlie.'

Emma realised she was rambling and took a deep breath before continuing. 'Two things I wanted to ask. Was the cottage left with contents or did someone else inherit them? I understand there were some good pieces, antiques I presume.'

'You'd better come through. I'm not sure if

I am really authorised to help you but I'll take a look at the file.' He led her through a narrow corridor into the depths of the building.

'Take a seat,' he told her. 'I'll get the details out.'

She sat opposite a large desk, covered in papers and with a computer monitor at one side. He took out a fat file and began to leaf through it, then he looked up at her, peering over narrow spectacles.

'You said there were two things you wanted to ask, but you only asked one thing.'

'Well, the doors were unlocked when I arrived so I sort of moved in. I've been staying there since last Thursday. Four nights, so far.'

'I see. But I thought you said the place had been stripped of the furniture?'

'Well yes. I bought a few basic necessities and I'm sort of camping out. There's an old iron bedstead and mattress so I have somewhere to sleep. Not that I'm getting much of that. I was really wondering if it's all right for me to be there? And if Charlie is really dead—not that I think she is—who does it belong to now?'

'Complicated. Well, as far as you staying there for the time being is concerned, since you were originally invited, I'm sure that is perfectly alright. Everything was signed and completed so it would be Charlotte's next of kin who would inherit, assuming she is herself intestate—hasn't made a will herself.'

106

'Knowing Charlie, that's most unlikely. What about the contents of Gull Cottage?'

'I suppose it will do no harm to tell you. The contents were included in the legacy so perhaps the police need to be informed if it's been cleared out. You are certain Charlotte herself hasn't already sold them?'

'Definitely. This was her first visit here and Martha was a distant relative she'd never even met before. In fact Charlie was really surprised to have inherited the place,' Emma said firmly.

'You say the place was unlocked when you arrived?'

'Yes. A neighbour had the keys and he said Martha never locked it so he didn't bother to lock it himself.'

'Perhaps that's a starting place to enquire, then. Not that I'm making any accusations, of course.'

'Did you ever visit the cottage?'

'No. Martha always came to the office to make her will and do any business she needed to do.'

'So few people would know what is actually missing? Nobody could identify the furniture even if it was found?'

'It's difficult to say. She must have had some friends, I suppose—she was quite a character. Very sad ending for her. Always so sprightly, one wouldn't have thought she was prone to accidents like that.'

'So I gather. And there was no investigation

into the possibility of anything . . . well, suspicious?'

'I don't think so. Apart from the Coroner's inquest of course. She was in her eighties after all. Old people do fall. Please let me know if you need any further help. Perhaps you could notify us if you hear of any outcome?'

'I will. Thank you very much. You've been more helpful than I could have hoped.'

'Not at all. I'll show you back to reception—it's a bit of a rabbit warren here.'

\*     \*     \*

Emma went back to the police station to collect her fully charged phone. Sam was at the desk, dealing with an elderly couple who seemed to have hearing difficulties. He smiled at her and nodded towards the seats. She down, waiting until at last the old folks left the station and she went forward.

'I've come to collect my phone.'

'No problem. Are you alright? I was worried when I heard you shouting and the phone went silent. How are you doing?'

'I'm OK. Grenville left me soon after but not without a number of threats. He was very edgy when I mentioned Martha's death. There's something suspicious involving him, I'm certain.'

'It was all tidied up after the inquest and the files closed. I'm not sure it can be taken any further.'

'I've just been to Martha's solicitor and he told me that the cottage contents were left to Charlie. They should all have been there so obviously, someone stripped the place, either sold the furniture or re-furnished their own house with it. I think that's terrible, and it must have been a bit of a shock for Charlie when she saw it. She would have known it should have been furnished from the terms of the will. I didn't see it of course, but I'm sure she's been robbed.'

'Yes indeed.'

'So you're admitting she probably did go there and see it?'

'Guess so, but I still have to question why she went down to the beach before doing anything about it.'

'I know, but Charlie is always impulsive. Maybe she went down to give herself time to think.'

'Sounds unlikely, but you know your friend. But all of this makes no difference if she did drive back up the A30. She may have had a reason.'

'But now we know it was a deliberate fire, doesn't that make it more likely that it was stolen and someone wanted to get rid of a body?'

'Look, they're still trying to identify the driver,' Sam told her. 'CID are taking over the case now. I'll tell the detectives you're still here and they might take a new statement from you, ask what you know about Charlie's dentist, credit cards and so on. Hang around and I'll see if they'll speak to you now.'

Emma sat down again. Things might be moving at last, it seemed. At least one positive had come out of it—it seemed they might be considering that it might not have been Charlie in the car. Nobody was any nearer knowing what had really happened, though, and Charlie was still missing.

Sam came back with a woman in civvies, not uniform.

'This is detective sergeant Eva Thompson. Eva, this is Emma Peterson. Charlotte's friend I told you about.'

'How do you do, Miss Peterson. Come on through, will you?' Emma followed the woman into the now familiar corridor and into another interview room exactly like the others. She sat at the familiar table and waited for the familiar questions.

'I've read your statement and the report of your previous visits. I can understand you're very anxious about your friend, but we still have to make certain that it was not her in the car. Once we've done that, we'll begin to treat this as a missing person case. But you must understand that we cannot devote endless time to an adult missing person. None of us know if she's gone off on her own and simply doesn't want to be found.'

'No, no, that's ridiculous, Charlie wouldn't do that. She had no reason to. She's a happy person, always a fun seeker and my very good friend. She knew I was on my way down to join her. Believe me, she wouldn't go willingly into hiding.'

'OK. I follow your thoughts. We'll probably do a check on her mobile phone and credit cards and her bank account, see when and if she last used it. Do you know where she banked?'

'I know she had an account with Mid-West, and I think she had a credit card with them, too. I saw her use it more than once. Many more times than was good for her, if the truth be told.' Emma smiled, remembering the mad shopping sprees she and Charlie had shared.

'Good. That's helpful and we can check on that. Now, her parents,' the detective said. 'I understand they live in Spain but you don't know where.'

'That's correct.' At least this woman had read her statements carefully, Emma thought.

'You don't think there's any chance she might have gone to see them? Had an urgent call if one of them was ill?'

'No. I'm sure she wouldn't have gone without telling me. We're very close and see each other all the time. Besides, like I said, I was on my way down here to join her. She'd hardly have disappeared without telling me. Not if she was able to call me.'

'So what do you think has happened to her?'

'I've simply no idea. I can't even speculate.'

'She's never done anything like this before? Disappeared, I mean,' the detective said carefully.

'Of course not.'

'Thank you. Well, we're sending someone to her home, a flat I believe it is. They'll gain access and see if they can find her parent's address, and anything else that might help us with the identification.'

'Do you have to tell her parents? I mean, is it kind to worry them if she's simply just gone away somewhere?'

'But you don't seem to think she has. We may leave it for a day or two, until we've checked on a few more things.'

'This identity thing. Would it help if I saw the . . . the remains? I may recognise something—or definitely not recognise something?' Emma offered tentatively.

'I'm afraid not. There's nothing left to recognise and it would only be very upsetting for you. Believe me, even when you're hardened to such sights, it can be most disturbing. Now, do you think there's anything else you have to tell us?'

'I'm not sure how relevant it is, but the cottage she inherited, Gull Cottage at Bodilly Cove . . . well, she was left the contents as well, but it's been cleared. It's empty of everything but a couple of old beds and a battered old chair. According to someone who knew Martha, the old lady, there were some good antiques there. And it also seems questionable that the old lady died as the result of a fall and then gas poisoning, since she was very healthy and not at all prone to falls.'

'But old people often do trip. I don't think there were any questions asked at the time, but I'll take a look at the file anyway. Thank you, Miss Peterson. We'll keep you informed.'

'Thank you. There's one more thing. I was going to ask the man who works in the shop at the garage at the top of Bodilly Cove Lane if he had sold the postcard to Charlie. If he saw her, he might remember her. He was away at some surf competition at the weekend. I thought I'd call on him later this evening.'

'You can leave all of that to us now, thank you.'

'His name is Colin. Colin James and he lives in Langton.'

'Right. Thank you for that.' She made a note. 'Leave it to us now, as I say. I'll send someone round to question him.'

Emma could think of nothing else to say so followed Eva Thompson to the door. She felt slightly comforted that she had finally got a positive reaction but completely frustrated that she now had to wait for someone else to do something. The two women shook hands and she went back into the reception area, where Sam was still at the desk.

He smiled at her. 'Any use?'

'I really don't know. She said I wasn't to do anything else and they would continue enquiries. But it's so hard to just sit and wait. Did I tell you that the furniture should all have been left in the cottage?'

'You did. I suppose Mum might remember some of the pieces. I suspect they're long gone now. I'll see if I can check any of the local auctions in the past few weeks but I don't hold out much hope. I suppose Rob is a prime suspect but we have no evidence apart from the fact he was a key holder. He'd deny everything of course and we've already upset him by visiting his house. Heavens, was it only this morning?'

'It does all seem a long time ago, doesn't it? Anyway, the solicitor says I'm alright to stay at the cottage for a while and my phone's charged again, so I'm at least able to contact people.'

'I'll come round this evening. How about I bring some fish and chips round?'

'I'm sure you've got better things to do than babysit me.'

'Not at all. I'll see Mum after work and see if she can remember anything about Martha's furniture.'

'Thanks. You could always bring her with you. Maybe if she's actually in the house, it could jog her memory. Mind you, she'd have to sit on the floor.'

'I'll bring some picnic chairs. Mum would enjoy that, I'm sure. OK, it's a date. I'll see you later. Meantime, don't do anything silly. No going off on your own and making enquiries that could get you into some sort of trouble.'

'I won't. I've had two serious scares already today. Not sure what I will do with the rest of the day though. I may just go for a quiet walk.'

'Good idea. Enjoy the scenery. See you later.'

Sam waved her goodbye as he answered the phone.

* * *

Emma drove back to Bodilly Cove and stopped again at the garage. She went into the office and asked if she could keep the hire car for a few more days.

'No problem,' Harry told her. 'You managing alright with it? I could let you have a better one if you want. I've got another one free at the moment.'

'It's fine thank you. I'm not actually doing much driving but it's convenient to have it.'

'You heard any more about that friend of yours? Bad business all round, that was,' Harry said.

'The police seem to think someone else could have been driving her car, but we still don't know what happened to my friend. I suppose she didn't come here? A yellow mini

115

with a black roof.'

'We had a yellow mini in here couple of Saturdays back. I remembered it when I read that report in the paper. Blonde girl, nice looking. She filled up with petrol and said she'd driven down and made it all the way here on one tank. Pleased she was.'

'That's Charlie. I'm sure of it. What time of day was it?'

'Oh, I couldn't be sure. Probably around lunchtime? Maybe early afternoon?'

'At least that's proof she actually got here. How did she pay for the petrol?' Emma asked in excitement. It was more proof she hadn't thought to check on and she kicked herself. Why hadn't she thought to ask before?

'Can't remember. Credit card I expect. Most people do.'

'I expect the police will be round to ask at some point. They're checking on her credit cards to try to see if they can find any information.'

'Thanks for the warning. I'll make sure everything's in order if they're coming nosing round.'

'Thank you. I can't tell you how pleased I am to get this news. In fact I think I'll celebrate with one of those delicious pasties.'

Harry watched until Emma had left the office and picked up the phone. He dialled a number and spoke quietly into it.

'I may be getting a visit from the police

soon. That's right. I'll be very careful, of course.'

Emma went into the shop, her whole body language much lighter and her smile back on her face.

'Hello Lucinda. I'd like one of your pasties, please,' she said almost happily.

'Now there's someone who's had some good news. Don't tell me they've found your friend?'

'Well no, but we can at least prove she came down here and that it's not likely to be her in the car. She bought petrol here, Harry told me.'

'So who was it in the car?'

'The police don't know yet. But it was set on fire deliberately, they say. Looks like it was stolen by someone. We don't know where it was taken from or where it went, since there's no way of telling how much petrol was left in it as it was burnt out.'

'Goodness me. To think it was right here in our garage and we never knew it.' She shook her head and tutted. 'And are you managing alright at the cottage?'

'Well, sort of. It's pretty basic but at least the weather's good so it doesn't matter too much. I can spend time outside.'

Emma paid for the pasty and said goodbye to Lucinda before she drove down the lane and stopped in the small car park where the start of the track to the cove began. She ate her pasty and looked around as if she was expecting some sort of clue to suddenly pop up.

Was this where Charlie had come to that fateful Saturday? She frowned. Everything she had worked towards was simply to prove Charlie had arrived here earlier in the day that Saturday. The fire had taken place in the evening. When she thought about it, what was there to say Charlie hadn't driven back up the A30 to where the car was found? Perhaps something had happened to make her drive back that way and it had been her friend in the car, after all.

The thought was unbearable after her recent hopes. Unable to face going back to the cottage, she decided on a walk along the coast. There was nothing she needed to do and now she had her phone re-charged, she would always be in communication if they needed to contact her.

Emma walked along the coastal path towards the east, the opposite way to Sam's village, passing Rob's cottage, slightly above the path. She glanced at it, keeping low against the hedge in case he was around and would call out something. There seemed to be a large amount of land around his cottage, mostly rough, uncultivated ground with several outbuildings, all in a tumbledown, un-cared for state. Knowing how keen people were to buy up such properties for re-development, he could be sitting on a potential fortune, if he had the intelligence to use it.

It was hot and Emma had come along somewhat unprepared and with no water. She wondered if she should go back or walk on to the next village, but decided to continue and try her best to enjoy the afternoon.

Wasn't this what she and Charlie had planned, after all? Rounding a corner, she could see a long stretch of the coast ahead. It was a perfect view with deep blue sea stretching endlessly and distant vistas of coastal villages and picturesque coastline. Purple bell heather was beginning to fade into russet colours and a few remaining pink flowers showed on dark green tussocks. It must be the thrift she'd read about and seen pictures of when it was in full flower, lining the whole area with brilliant pink.

She heard voices as people were approaching.

'Lovely afternoon,' called the man leading the family group.

'Yes,' Emma said, pleased to have human contact again. 'Do you know how far it is to the next village?'

'I'm sorry, I don't. The path goes up and down so much, it's quite hard to tell. There's a lane leading up to the main road a bit further back but it's quite a hike.'

'Have to keep motivating the kids with promises of ice cream and such like. Oh, well, ever onwards. Enjoy your day.'

'Thanks. And you.'

Emma watched as they walked out of sight. Presumably, mother and father and two young teenagers, perhaps, carefree and enjoying a holiday. She sighed enviously and continued along her way, eventually coming to a steep drop in the path and debated whether or not to go down. If she did, it would be a steep climb back up again, but it did look as if there was some sort of building down there and may even be some sort of shop where she could buy some water. The pasty had left her feeling quite thirsty, so she began the climb down.

As she approached, Emma could see a long low building with a black roof. There were people sitting outside doing something she couldn't see but there was a strong smell of something fishy. She remembered someone saying there was a fish processing place here so this must be it. She hadn't thought about it before, but realised the crab and shrimps that were in many shops around, had to be picked over, shells removed and the flesh taken out.

As she got closer, she could see a row of women with piles of shrimps and prawns, peeling them and tossing unwanted parts into huge plastic tubs. They were chatting to each other in a language she didn't understand. Most of them were also wearing scarves over their heads, reminding her of the women she had seen that morning in her garden. Maybe these people were the very ones she had seen but if so, they had learned their skills very quickly. She watched their nimble fingers working at great speed and smiled at them as she walked past. They acknowledged her but nobody spoke to her.

There was a small harbour with two or three small and elderly looking fishing boats moored against a jetty. She saw there were a few houses slightly inland and left the coast to see if there was a shop. It was little more than a shed but was selling cold drinks, ices and a few beach toys. Obviously it only opened during the summer season.

She stopped at the hatch and asked for a bottle of water. 'You on holiday then?' asked the young woman in a disinterested way.

'Yes, I suppose I am,' Emma answered. She could hardly say anything else. 'I'll have an ice cream as well please. The good weather must help your trade.'

'S'pose, though there's not been much trade yet even though it's July. I'm only here for the school holidays. Then I'm hoping I go to college. What flavour did you want?'

'Vanilla's fine, thanks. You don't work for the fish people then?' Emma asked.

'Nah. Too stingy they are. Don't pay us locals anythin'. Why should they when all them foreigners come over and work for next to nothin'?'

'I suppose they stay in the village, do they?'

'Dunno. A mini bus comes to collect them and brings them in each mornin'. They're usually here by the time I get here. That's two pounds and tenpence,' she said.

Emma handed the coins over.

'Thanks. If I go inland, are there any buses back along towards Bodilly Cove?'

'Yeah, but not very regular. Don't say you're staying there?'

'Well yes, why?'

'Got a bad reputation that area.'

'So I keep hearing.'

'Just take care, that's my advice.'

'Thanks again. I will.'

*Someone else warning me off*, she thought. How peculiar. Emma sat and ate her ice cream, thinking she was getting into bad habits—ice cream, pasties, fish and chips.

Once she'd finished, she couldn't face the steep climb back and walked inland, hopefully towards a road where the buses ran. Eventually she saw a bus shelter and looked at the timetable. There was one due in half an hour so she decided to wait. She looked round the village, such as it was. A few houses and a pub and little else. It seemed a rather depressing place and not the picturesque fishing port it may once have been, so she went back to the bus stop and sat to wait.

There were few passengers on the bus and it was just a short journey back to the garage, where she got off and walked down the lane to where she had left her car, feeling a slight sense of relief to see it was still there. With all she kept hearing about the area, it seemed nothing could be guaranteed.

When she drove back to the farm entrance, Mrs Crelly was in the garden and waved her down.

'Hello dear. You were supposed to be coming in for a cuppa today. Did you forget?'

'Oh, I'm sorry. Yes, I did forget. I was in Penzance this morning and then I went for a walk.'

'Well come on in now. The kettle's just boiled and I've got some fresh scones just out of the oven.'

'Well, that's kind of you, but I . . .'

'No excuses. Come and tell me what's been going on. You've been in and out of that cottage like a yoyo.'

'OK, thank you. I've been desperately trying to find out what happened to my friend, Charlie. I know she definitely came here on that Saturday afternoon, even if you didn't see her. She got petrol at the garage, and the postcard she sent to me and she went for a walk on the beach. But the police don't know what happened after that.'

'Really? You've been very busy to find out all of that. Now, help yourself.'

Mrs Crelly poured tea and put a plate of scones and homemade jam before her. Having recently eaten the pasty and an ice cream, eating was the last thing in the world she needed, but Emma politely took one and made comments about how delicious they were. After a further spell of small talk, she asked one of her burning questions.

'Do you know what happened to Martha's furniture and all the contents of the cottage?'

The woman looked away, avoiding eye contact.

'I expect they were sold by the solicitors,' she said looking slightly uncomfortable, or so Emma thought.

'No, I visited them today. The contents were left to my friend, along with the property.'

'Really? Not easy to take stuff out of there, the cottage being placed where it is. Not like anyone could get a van very close.'

'Perhaps it was looted a bit at a time. Seems it was left unlocked most of the time since Martha's death. You were a friend of hers weren't you? You must have been inside and seen her things?'

'Well, yes. I often went to see her. We used to get shopping and stuff for her. Martha was a great walker though and used to go off on the bus every week, so we just took the heavy stuff. Her oil and gas for the cooker got delivered to us.'

'It's a bit of an inconvenient place for most things isn't it?'

'For you modern young ladies, I'm sure it is.

124

I'm surprised you're sticking it out there.'

'I can't leave until I know what happened to my friend, and I need to know what's happened to all the contents of the cottage, for Charlie's sake. Rob Grenville was given a key to pass on to Charlie when she arrived, but I wondered if he had a key already. Someone's been going into the cottage and moving my stuff around, you see.'

'Kids maybe? There's a few around on the campsites just along the way a bit.'

'But I always lock the door before I leave the place. I've been locking up everywhere very carefully, in fact.'

'Sounds like you're being attacked by the ghosts of the old sailors lost down in the Cove. It has a bit of a reputation.'

'So I gather. People always get a strange look on their faces when anyone mentions Bodilly Cove. But ghosts? I don't think so. I don't believe in ghosts,' Emma said with a smile.

'Can't go saying things like that. Just 'cos you haven't seen one doesn't mean they don't exist.'

'Maybe not.'

'Come on now. Eat up.'

'Thank you. I've had plenty. I have to confess to eating a pasty and an ice cream not so long ago. And I should be getting back, I've delayed you long enough.'

'Not at all. I'm glad you seem happier about

125

your friend. Terrible business, it was.'

'Oh, I almost forgot. Sam Henley and his mother are visiting me tonight. Is it alright for them to drive across the field?'

'Sam the policeman?' Emma nodded. 'I dare say Mr Crelly won't mind. Ground's still dry. He won't be so pleased when the rains come, though.'

'Thanks. Perhaps you can mention it him? I promise you, it isn't the start of me having a load of visitors. Mrs Henley used to visit Martha and we thought she might be able to describe some of the missing furniture. Then we can look around some of the second hand stores to see if any of it's there.'

'I expect you'll be lucky to see any of it again,' she said a trifle sharply.

'What makes you say that?' asked Emma as politely as she could in spite of her sudden feeling of foreboding.

'Just that things go missing round here, too many strangers come and go. Oh, did you need that phone of yours charging?'

'I got it charged this morning. I did knock to take you up on your kind offer but got no reply. I expect you were out in the fields,' Emma suggested.

'More likely in the milking parlour or the barn. We're a bit short handed at present so I have a few extra things to do.'

'I did look over there but . . . well, you weren't around so I persuaded someone at the

126

police station to charge it for me.'

'That's good. Keep me posted now, won't you?'

'I will. Thanks.'

Emma drove away, feeling certain Mrs Crelly was hiding something. Her mood had definitely changed when Emma had mentioned the furniture.

She remembered the boxes and covered shapes in the barn. Perhaps some of the furniture was being stored there? She might try to take a look if the chance arose.

Parking in her usual place, Emma climbed through the fence. The gate was hanging open, as was the door. She walked up the path cautiously, calling out as she reached the door.

# CHAPTER 8

Emma looked inside but all seemed to be as she had left it, except for the open door. She was certain she had locked it. Gripping her bag once more to use as a weapon if she needed it, she looked around. The living room, which she never used, looked exactly as she had last seen it. She went up the stairs cautiously, silently, and looked into the bedroom. Quite what she would have done if anyone was there, she didn't know.

She looked into the other bedroom but

that too was as she had left it. Someone was seriously trying to make her more nervous. It had to be Rob Grenville, she reasoned. He had threatened her that morning and for whatever reason, seemed not to want her around. All seemed well so she gave a shrug and went back downstairs.

She went outside and looked around. Everything seemed just as she had left it. She went up the garden to what she thought of as the loo and all was well there. She didn't leave anything of value in the house so just had to accept that all was well. She sat on the old armchair and waited. She picked up her book and began to read. She actually fell asleep after a little while and woke to hear someone calling her.

'Hello?' she called out loud.

'Hi. We're just on the other side of your hedge. Is it OK to come through?' It was Sam and his mother.

'Oh, yes, of course. Can I help?'

'Thanks, yes. If you could help Mum through the hedge, I'll then pass the chairs.'

Emma helped his mother to climb through and then took charge of the chairs. Sam handed her the rest of the things and then climbed through himself. They all walked down the path and into the cottage.

'Welcome, such as it is . . .' Emma said.

'Oh dear. It isn't how I remembered it,' she said. 'It looks sort of forgotten. Very sad.'

128

'I was hoping you would remember something . . . anything, to make it seem like what it used to be.'

'I'm sorry. I really am. Let's sit outside and eat the fish and chips first and maybe something will come to me.'

'Come on, Mum,' Sam said. 'You sit here and I'll hand out the food.' He turned to Emma. 'I assume you've got vinegar?'

Emma shook her head.

'Oh well, never mind. Tuck in and enjoy.'

They all three sat on the picnic chairs and ate, chatting as they did, and when they were finished, Sam collected the papers together and they started their tour of the cottage.

His mother, Joan, made comments as they walked round.

'Those beds are different. I know I only saw them for a while, but they were definitely different, with proper headboards and pretty floral covers.'

'So, what do you think happened to them?' Emma asked. She felt relieved, in a way, that Charlie's Aunt Martha hadn't been forced to sleep in these beds.

'Whatever's happened to the rest of the furniture, I suppose,' replied Joan. 'Oh dear, I feel like an intruder.'

'Don't be silly, Mum,' Sam told her. 'It's hardly your fault now, is it? What we need to do is to try to make a list of what's missing. Everything you can think of, Mum.'

'Alright. There's the dresser, of course. That used to stand over there near the door, against that wall. And there was always the kitchen table.'

'What do you mean?' Emma asked.

'Well, this one is hardly the one that Martha used. This is tiny, but hers almost filled the room. Well, not really, but it was much bigger than this one. And this one is almost falling apart.'

'I see. So someone has taken the proper table away and left this one instead?'

'Yes. I'm certain of it.'

For the next half hour, Sam's mother went round the cottage, pointing at various spots and telling them what was missing. Sam was making careful notes and paused every now and again to ask about details.

'So, it looks as though everything that should have been here isn't here and someone has taken it away and replaced a lot of it with cheap nasty stuff instead. Hmm . . . interesting. I wonder why they put this stuff back in here?'

'I expect they heard Charlie and I were coming down.' Emma felt quiet for a moment or two. 'I suppose they felt as if something would happen if there was nothing at all left here.'

'Maybe. I should think they hoped Charlie would simply go away again and they could easily take charge of the place.'

Emma made coffee for everyone, using

the picnic cups from her set. They went to sit outside again and planned what they might need to do.

'I really don't think you should continue to stay here alone, dear,' said Sam's mother. 'I think you should pack up and come to stay with us.'

'I can't. Really, I can't. Suppose Charlie calls me here? I need to be around if she does.'

'You could come back with us. Seriously, you could,' added Sam. 'Your phone will still work at our place. And if anyone comes along to terrorise you, you'll be safe with us. Don't treat these guys without respect for what they might do.'

'I'm not. I'll stay tonight and see about coming to you tomorrow. I just feel I need to be here tonight. I'm not sure why.'

'I give up on you. You're potty, do you realise that?' Sam added sharply. He felt annoyed with her for not taking care with her own preservation.

'I'm sorry, but please, don't think I'm not grateful. It's nice to know there's someone who cares about me.'

'I doubt there's much more to say. I suppose we should be getting back now. It's starting to get quite late. I'll take our rubbish with us. Won't leave stuff for you to get rid of.'

'Right. I'll have to help you, of course.'

They carried the chairs back to the hedge and Sam climbed through the fence. Emma passed him the chairs and turned to get the bag of rubbish. She felt saddened at the prospect of being alone again and, though she didn't admit it, slightly nervous. So she kept smiling bravely and hoped nothing was showing in her expression.

'Right, I think that's the lot. You really sure you won't come?' Sam asked her.

'I am. Thanks though. Thank you both. I'll be fine now and I'll call you in the morning. What time suits you best?'

'Whenever. I don't mind being woken early.'

'Goodbye, dear,' Joan added. 'I'm really sorry to be leaving you behind.'

'Thank you again,' Emma said, 'Thank you both for coming and for being so kind.'

She watched as they drove back up the field, leaving her little car behind them. She turned back to the house and rinsed out the cups. It was almost ten o'clock, so she thought she might as well go to bed. After the early start, it was the most sensible thing to do, after all.

She locked up carefully and slipped the chair against the door, knowing that it would take considerable force to move it—and make a lot of noise if it was attempted.

She fell asleep quickly and slept right through until the next morning. She had survived another night. Stretching and yawning, she decided to get up. She staggered down the stairs and washed in the sink.

It was six thirty and still pretty early to be

up and about, so she put some coffee on and opened the door, but it was very damp outside and she gave a shiver, thinking that maybe staying in was the best thing to do, so she came back inside and sat in the large chair to drink her coffee.

It was Tuesday and she had been here, on her own, for five nights. She contemplated Sam's advice. In many ways, it would be better if she moved away and went to stay with them but something was keeping her here. She needed to call him to let him know she was safe again this morning but decided to leave it until later. Maybe she should go for a walk?

Emma locked up the cottage and set off down the cliff path, towards the cove at the base of it. She felt thoughtful and had almost decided to go and take up Sam and Joan's offer to stay with them. She sat on a rock at the bottom of the cliff and watched as the waves rolled back and forth for a while before she glanced at her watch and decided to go back to the cottage.

Halfway up, her phone beeped; a message arrived, so she stopped to look.

*Hi Hun. I've decided to sell the cottage. Go back home. Sorry! Love Charlotte.*

What on earth was that about? The message had come from Charlie's phone but it was certainly not the sort of message she usually sent. Hun? That was weird. As was her name, Charlotte. She never used it except to sign cheques or formal letters. She would certainly never use it to send a text message. What was going on? Why had Charlie sent her this message?

She climbed back up the cliff to the top and paused a moment to catch her breath before she dialled Sam's phone.

'Hello? Sam, it's me.'

'Hi Emma. What's up?'

'I've just got a text from Charlie. Well, from her phone, but it's weird. Not at all the type of thing she'd send to me. I can't really believe it.'

'What does it say?'

Emma repeated it to him. 'Hun is wrong. She never calls me that. And she's signed it Charlotte. What should I do?'

'Stay right where you are. I'll come round immediately.'

Sam switched off his phone and she sat waiting. Would he come by car or along the coastal path? The latter would be quickest but she would need to wait and see. She decided to eat something but when she looked at the bread, it had gone mouldy. She would have to buy some later, but meanwhile, her hunger pains would have to wait.

At last, Sam arrived, along the coastal path, riding his scooter.

'Morning. You're certainly keeping someone busy.'

'Morning. Sorry to drag you along here.'

'That's not a problem. Now, can I see the

message you received?' She handed the phone over, having placed the message on the screen. 'I wonder who sent it?' he mused.

'I suspect Charlie did, but I really can't believe she would have sent something so stupid, with so many mistakes. I think she was being forced to send it to get me out of the way. I did try to call her but the phone was dead again.'

'I'll have to tell Eva. They're checking on calls sent from her phone. Don't look so worried. Hey, come on.'

Sam put his arm across Emma's shoulder and gave her a comforting squeeze.

'I really don't know what's going on,' Emma sighed.

'Of course you don't, but I really do think you should move. Why don't you pack all your stuff up and move along to our place? Leave the cottage empty?'

'But suppose Charlie comes back? She'll expect to find me here,' Emma protested.

'I know, but . . . look, come over anyway and spend the day with Mum. She'd love to have you there with her. I have to work of course, but you'd at least have someone to talk to.'

'I don't know . . . I'll think about it.'

'You won't. I'm sorry, but I'm going to insist. You get what you need for the day and get into the car. I'll go back along the path and I'll meet you at the other end.'

'But you'll be late for work,' she protested.

135

'I can phone and tell them I've seen you and that I'll be coming in with some new information.'

'OK, thanks. Thanks a lot, Sam. Sorry I've been bumbling along so badly. I'll get my bag organised and I'll get on my way.'

'Make sure you do,' Sam told her firmly, then added,

'And lock up. I'll get back and let Mum know to expect you.'

Emma packed her shoulder bag with her book and a cardigan. She didn't have anything else but left her travel bag tucked under the sink. She wasn't sure why she did it but felt it was safer than left out in the room. She looked around and locked up, trapping the paper into the door as she closed it. She went to get into her car and set off up the field.

As she got out to open the gate, she saw the farmer.

'You going home then?' said Mr Crelly.

'Home? Oh no, I'm just going out for the day. I'll be back later.' She gave him a wave as she got back into the car. 'Bye. I'll maybe see you when I'm coming back.'

He stared after her and scowled. What was she up to? He didn't like her crossing his fields like this. Maybe he should say something to make her stop.

\*　　　\*　　　\*

As she drove towards the next village, Emma was thinking hard. Sam had the information he needed and would take it into the police station. She could go herself but hopefully it might not be necessary. She must ask Sam what he thought about it.

She turned down the lane where he lived and saw his car still parked outside.

'Everything alright?' he asked.

'I think so. You are sure your mum doesn't mind?'

'Of course not. Now, off you go inside and she'll feed you. I'm going to work now, but keep your phone handy. I'll tell the CID people about your call and they might want to see you. Maybe not, but we'll see. Bye for now.'

'Thanks a lot. I'll speak to you later.'

Emma watched as he drove away and then turned to knock at the door.

'Come away in, dear. I've got some bacon and eggs on their way and some toast. Anything else you'd like?'

'That sounds wonderful. Thank you so much.'

'So, tell me. What happened to you this morning? You can tell me while breakfast's cooking, won't be long now.'

Emma told her everything that had happened since the previous night and even showed her the text in question.

'So, you see, I'm very much in your debt. I

needed to come here and spend the day with you. But if you have things to do, perhaps I might do something to help?'

'Bless you, dear. Now, here we go. You enjoy this.'

'I'm starving! Thank you again.'

Emma ate hungrily; she didn't realise how much she had needed this and was very grateful.

They chatted easily and never mentioned the problems she'd had. During the rest of the morning, Joan got on with her cleaning, talking as she did so. It was pleasant and relaxing.

'Please, let me do something to earn my keep?' she asked.

'I've got to go shopping in a while. Do you want to come with me?' Joan suggested.

'That would be really nice.'

So once Joan had finished her cleaning, they went to town in Emma's car and parked in the supermarket car park. She couldn't believe she wasn't needed and trailed round behind Joan, looking at things on the shelves and generally pushing the trolley round for the woman. This was actually quite grim, even though her hostess chatted away happily.

By the time they were going home, Emma realised that this was not the sort of day she really wanted, so she helped Joan to unload the shopping and finally said, 'I think I might just go to visit the museum in town. I hope you don't think I'm rude?'

'That's alright dear. I am assuming you'll some back here for some supper with us?'

'If you don't mind. Thank you, that would be lovely. I'll be back before too long.'

Emma drove away from the house, thinking how desperately boring she was being. She was on her way back into Penzance when her phone rang, so she pulled over to one side of the road and stopped.

'Hello?' she said cautiously.

'Is that Emma? It's Eva Thompson. I was wondering if we could call on you? A few things I need to ask you.'

'I can come into the office if you like. I'm nearly in Penzance.'

'OK, that would be great. Can you remember the way into the car park?'

'Yes thanks. I should be with you in about five or ten minutes.'

Emma re-started her car and drove in towards the town, feeling comforted at the thought of doing something. She drove to the police station and into the parking space at the side.

'Hello. I'm here at the request of Eva Thompson.'

'Take a seat will you please.'

The current desk officer was younger than Sam and seemed quite flustered. He pressed a couple of buttons and spoke.

'What's your name?' he asked. She told him and he repeated it into the phone.

A few seconds later and a woman came to show her through.

'Eva Thomson is just finishing something with another client. She'll see you in a moment or two. Come this way. Take a seat here. She won't keep you for a moment or two.'

Emma sat uncomfortably on the hard bench. The door opened and a man in his twenties came out, looked at her and gave her a glare. Emma tried to smile but he looked away and walked off along the corridor. She shrugged and looked at the door and waited . . . and waited. Surely Eva would come out soon, she thought. After a few minutes longer, Eva came out at last.

'Sorry to keep you. Please come in.'

'Who was that?' she asked.

'Colin James. Did you know him?'

'Not at all. He just looked at me as if he could . . . well, who can say?'

'Well now, I understand from Sam that you had a call or message from Charlie this morning?'

'Well yes, but it was very strange . . .'

'May I see it, do you think?'

'Here it is.' She handed her phone to the DS. After a few moments, she asked, 'So what do you think?'

'What do *you* think?'

'I don't believe it's genuine, I really don't. The thing is, she'd never call me "Hun" and she'd never sign with "Love, Charlotte." She's always Charlie, never Charlotte.'

'So you think that she might have been made to do it?'

'I suppose. But she would have put something else in there rather than that.'

'OK. I'm inclined to agree with you. We've actually been hunting for the number. It's only been used once in the past few days. We believe it came from the Falmouth region. If that's so, why do you think she might have gone there?'

'Falmouth? Where's that?'

'Along the coast from you, a little further East. We're just confused about the whereabouts. Do you know if she would be in Falmouth, and why?'

'I've no idea at all. Sorry. This is all getting rather weird, isn't it?' Emma said, frustrated.

'Well, yes. I can see what you mean. If you think of anything else to report to us, let us know. Thanks for coming in.'

'That's alright.' She rose and paused. 'What has been going on with Colin? I mean, did you get anything out of him? About Charlie, I mean.'

Eva smiled. 'Nothing really. He claims not to have seen Charlie. I can't hold him here so I've had to let him go.'

'Oh, I see. Well, thanks for being honest with me. Is there anything else?'

'I don't think so. Not for now, anyway.'

'Have you done any DNA tests on the body

in the car?'

'Well yes. It proves she was an immigrant.

'Really? That's quite something then, isn't it?'

'It is an interesting development and we now have to search for your friend. Look, I'm sorry, but I am very busy. I'll keep you posted with information when we get it. Thanks again.'

Emma went out to the corridor and someone came along to return her to the outside world again. Or what she saw as the outside world. Emma looked around to see if Sam was anywhere but he wasn't. She would see him later.

She went outside and back to her car. As she was about to get into it, Colin came round the corner and stopped beside her.

'Leave me out of this mess, will ya? Dunno what you were saying but leave me alone. Get it?'

'I'm sorry,' she replied. 'What's your problem with me?'

'Gettin' me dragged in there. I didn't want to go but they made me. Just you forget all about me, understand?'

He turned and left her sitting in her car as he rushed off down the road and disappeared.

Well, well, Emma thought. So that's the delightful Colin is it? Thoughtfully, she started her car and set off down to the harbour. She drove along a little way and saw a road turning back towards the main road. She drove along it and was soon on her way back to the village she had left behind her, some while ago. She stopped at Sam's house but sat and waited in the car for a moment.

'Oh, it's you. Glad you're safe. Come on in and have a cup of tea. I was just about to make one for myself.' Joan said when she saw her.

'Oh, thank you Mrs—Joan. That's kind of you.'

'No need to thank me. Now, come and take the weight off your feet. I need a bit of a sit down, don't you?'

She did prattle on, Emma thought, but she was very sweet. As they drank their tea, there was a constant stream of questions, which Emma tried to answer as best as she could. It was all to do with the saga and Joan kept saying, 'well, well, well.' Emma hoped to goodness that Sam came home soon. Then they could have a break from it all and maybe talk about something different.

At last, Sam did arrive home and brought some flowers to keep his mother happy. She was very taken with them and went off to the kitchen to put them into a vase.

'So, what's new?' Sam asked.

'Nothing really. I don't think Eva accepted what I said about this supposed text message. She said it was made in Falmouth and I said I didn't know anything at all about Falmouth but she seemed to think Charlie is still there.'

'I've been over there this afternoon. That's where I was when you came into the police station. No joy there anyway. We're stuck again, as ever.'

'Oh dear. That's sad.'

'It is rather. Can I get you a drink?'

'White wine would be good, if you have any.'

'White wine, coming up. I'll get some for Mum as well, then leave her inside, cooking.'

'That's wicked.'

'I know. Good, isn't it? Back in a mo.'

Emma sat still and thought about it all. She had been overjoyed, very briefly, but now, it all had fizzled into a nothing that she couldn't help with.

If someone else had sent the text, they were obviously holding Charlie against her will, but where though? And what had they done to her?


# CHAPTER 9

It had been a long day. At nine thirty, Emma decided she would return home again, refusing the pleas of the Henleys to stay with them instead.

'I just feel that I really need to be there somehow, but many thanks for the offer of help,' she told them.

'I don't like you being there alone. Look, why don't I come and stay with you? I can sleep in the second bedroom. I've got a sleeping bag, somewhere, haven't I, Mum?'

'Well yes, you have, dear. But . . .'

'No buts, I'm coming with you, Emma. I'll put some things into my car and follow you down the track. I assume the Crellys won't object?'

'I shouldn't think so, but are you really sure it's necessary? I mean to say, I . . .'

'I insist. I'll go and get my things. You stay where you are, won't be long.'

Emma helped clear the table and wash up. Sam's Mum wasn't too keen but she understood the need to keep moving, and when her son came back with a rucksack, she hurried them both away.

'Now, go on with you, both of you. Don't let anyone spoil the night with phone calls or anything else.'

'We won't,' Sam told her. 'Just you make sure you lock up safely here. Bye, Mum, take care.'

'It's alright. I was just carried away for a moment. I'll be fine. I'll make the coffee.'

Sniffing back her tears, Emma made two cups of coffee and handed one to Sam.

'It will be alright, won't it, Sam?'

'It will, I'm sure. Now, drink up and then take yourself upstairs to bed.'

145

It was six o'clock when Emma awoke the next day. She stretched and sat up, surprised that she'd had a remarkably good night's sleep. Then she remembered. She pulled on her top and shot downstairs to find Sam, still lying in the chair where she had left him the previous night.

He woke and looked at her strangely.

'Oh, heavens. I did fall asleep, eventually.' He smiled at her. 'Don't tell me you didn't sleep?'

'I did, actually, thank you. I'm sorry. I was expecting to come down and relieve you at some point. Do you want to go upstairs and get some sleep now?'

'No, it's alright. I think I'll see how the day goes. So, what's for breakfast?'

'Oh no, I forgot to buy more bread!' Emma gasped. 'I think there may be some eggs left.'

'You make it sound most appealing. We could go and find breakfast somewhere, I suppose.'

'That sounds like a much better idea. It's still early though.'

'I have to shave first, to get myself into working condition.'

'Well, the sink is all yours. I'll go into the garden and leave you to it.' It was her way of giving him some privacy. 'Unless you'd like some more coffee? I can make that first.'

146

'OK. We'll have some coffee first. I'm more than happy with that,' Sam said, smiling.

So Emma made some coffee and they went to sit on the step outside. It was another lovely day and she felt as if they were really on holiday and could have enjoyed a day on the beach, except for what was being threatened.

Just thinking about it made Emma felt sick again and she remembered the problems that lay ahead.

'What's up?' asked Sam, seeing her expression change.

'Nothing . . . everything . . . I really don't know what's going on. I feel sort of worried and anxious and then things seem to be getting better. Then it all crashes down again. Oh, I'm sorry. I shouldn't go on and on like this.'

'I'll get myself ready and we'll go and find some breakfast. You'll feel better after that.'

Sam got up and went inside to get himself ready, while Emma went up the garden to the shed for a while. By the time she came back and went inside, Sam was almost ready so she went to get herself dressed.

'There's that sleeping bag out there. I still need to find out what's in it,' she said to Sam in passing.

'I'll take a look. Don't worry about it, just you get yourself washed and dressed properly and I'll deal with it.'

She went inside and Sam went to look at the sleeping bag. Whatever it was that had been in it had now gone. It was dirty inside and not very pleasant and as he inspected it he decided that it was best thrown away.

'I'll take it away with me,' he told Emma.

*　　　*　　　*

It was a difficult morning.

They had breakfast in Penzance at a place where the men going out on the boats usually fed. It was cheap and cheerful and Sam insisted on paying.

Emma began to feel better after they'd eaten and went back with Sam to collect his things left at the cottage.

'I want you to go and see Mum again, today. I really think you should consider her offer to go and stay with her and leave this place empty of everything.'

'I'll really think about it, I promise. I refuse to let anyone frighten me away though. I'm not giving in to threats or anything else. I'm going to go for a walk along the coast again. I think the place along there, the fish farm place, is worth being investigated. I don't know why but I do think there's something happening there that may give us a clue.'

'You are not to go there on your own. Promise me, Emma.'

'I'm not going to go today, I promise you that much. But I have to go back again to look.'

'Emma, you really shouldn't go alone. Promise me.'

'OK, I promise, but you must realise that there's something odd about it.'

'I'll see if they'll let me go. Maybe if I go in uniform and make it look like it's something we're doing, it will be alright.'

'Thank you Sam. And I'm sorry I didn't let you sleep comfortably in my bed.'

'Now there's a thought . . .' Sam gave a wry grin and noticed with pleasure that it made Emma blush.

'Sorry,' she stammered. 'I meant that I was just thinking that you needed some sleep.'

'It's OK,' Sam smiled gently. 'I was just trying to make you smile a little.'

'Sorry. I'll go for a walk along the coastal path and clear my brain a bit. You go do whatever you need to do. And many thanks for staying here last night. I really do appreciate it. Now, go.'

'Ok. See you later. Please consider coming home to stay.'

'I will.'

Emma watched him drive away and went back inside the cottage, where she tidied up a bit and then decided to go for a walk along the cliff path towards the fish farm. She may have promised Sam that she wouldn't visit it on her own, but she wanted to see if the women were working there today.

She put her paper in the door, and locked it,

then set off along the cliff top.

As she was passing Rob Grenville's place, Emma heard voices. She recognised Rob as one of the people but the other, though it sounded vaguely familiar, she couldn't quite place.

'You stupid bastard. You've caused no end of trouble with your bumbling ways. Why couldn't you be satisfied with the way things were running?'

'Cos that bloody woman turned up. How could we carry on using Martha's place as a stop off when she was comin'?'

Emma froze. She pressed herself closer to the hedge, a stone wall with abundant gorse and other plants growing out of the top. She sat down slowly, scarcely daring to breathe.

'You didn't have to get rid of the old woman that way. That was the start of the trouble. She was always willing to help out. You just got greedy.'

'She was asking for more and more money for doing the bit she did. And what did she do for us anyways? A day and night for them to stay while we fixed the transport.'

'She gave them some food and a bit of comfort, sent them on their way a bit happier than when they landed. We never knew exactly when they'd arrive so it was convenient. You've buggered up everything. Yesterday's lot nearly brought the whole business crashing down.'

'It was that perishin' girl calling the cops. Your bloke din't tell us as he were comin' this time. I only just got them hid away in time.' That was Rob's voice.

'And the other one. If you hadn't done for Martha in the first place, she'd have still been there and everything would have gone on the same old way,' said the other man. He seemed to be more in charge of the operation.

'Nobody 'spected it were me. Accidental death, they said.'

'You were lucky. Very lucky.'

'Clever, I says. Not many ud of thought of putting the gas oven on. Finished her off that did.'

'Like I said. Lucky. But the whole business is getting dicey. Not helped by the dead woman turning up along with the previous shipment. Getting rid of her wasn't easy. Don't know why he didn't chuck her overboard before they landed. Still, it's done with now.'

'Lucky you managed to get the car to take them down towards the Lands End depot.'

'So, what you done with the other girl?'

'She's safe enough. Can't keep her hidden forever though. Think it will have to be a boat trip somewhere.'

Emma stuffed her hand against her mouth to stop herself crying out.

That man, whoever he was, had Charlie locked away somewhere. She felt like leaping up and challenging them but she would be risking her own safety, possibly even her life.

If only she'd thought of it, she could have recorded what they were saying on her phone. She pulled it out and tried to turn it to the recording device, but the voices had already died away. They were obviously walking back to the cottage.

Just faintly, she heard Rob's final orders given by the boss.

'Get rid of her. Do whatever it takes.'

Emma sat rigid with fear. She didn't dare to move in case Rob came back in that direction and saw her. She sat for half an hour or more until finally, all seemed quiet and she stood up.

There were more voices but this time It was holiday makers, walking along the path. Seeing normal people doing normal things made her feel as if she'd been dreaming. She nodded to them as she passed them but didn't feel like speaking to them.

In a dreamlike state, she walked back towards Gull Cottage. Should she phone Sam now and tell me what she had overheard? Would anyone believe her? Her mind was full of the things she had heard. Who was Rob talking to? Why did she think she might possibly recognise the voice of the other man?

Whoever it was, Rob was clearly implicated in some sort of people smuggling and also the murder of Martha. It was a murder after all but it would probably be impossible to prove.

Most of all, she was worried about Charlie.

Emma almost ran back to the cottage and went inside, dropping the door paper as she went inside. She needed to tell someone what she had heard. Should she go straight to the police station or should she simply phone to tell them? She didn't want to stay here any longer, so she would drive into the police station and tell them everything.

After that, she would come back and pack and leave this dreadful place. Whatever happened to it, she didn't much care. She wanted to find Charlie and go home with her. Leave all of this behind her.

Still shaking, Emma got into her car and drove up the bumpy field. What she had heard made her realise that she needed proper help. As she was passing the farm, she saw Mr Crelly standing looking over the gate. She gave him a wave and drove past him. He began to shout after her but she didn't stop; she knew she needed to get to the police station and tell them about what she had heard.

The officer she met at the police station took her details. She was sympathetic and listened to everything Emma had to say. She made no comments on her words but said she would take the notes to DS Thompson when she got back.

'Is that alright?' she asked Emma.

'I suppose so. Is Sam in yet?' Emma was troubled.

'No, I don't think so. Is there something

153

else?'

'No, not really. I'll go back home and start to pack up. I think I've stayed there long enough.'

'Very good. I think it's for the best.'

Emma left the police station and went back to the cottage. She would definitely pack up her things and go to stay with the Henleys. That was the best plan now.

# CHAPTER 10

Emma took her car though the Crelly's fields and went to the cottage. She felt tearful and upset about everything, but she knew it was the best plan. She stopped at the top of the drive when she saw that the door had been left open. Slowly, she walked towards the cottage.

It was a scene of chaos and devastation. Her clothes were tossed around, many of them ripped and spoiled. Her small food store was ruined, coffee thrown over everything and powdered milk added for good measure. Stale bread, butter and eggs were mashed into her clothes and the plastic picnic set was trampled and broken.

Tears of anger and frustration poured out and she shouted out loud, 'No. No. You can't get away with this!'

Emma had no doubt who had done it. Rob

was following his orders. Anything to drive her away. She ran upstairs to the bedroom and saw her bed had been ripped apart—he must have had a knife with him and used it to rip the fabric. Lying on top of it, as if trying to give her a message, was the sheet torn from the local paper with the photograph and report of the burnt car. It was giving her a clear threat: Look what happens if you stick around.

She pulled out her phone and pressed the button for Sam, but got his voice mail.

'Sam, someone's broken into the cottage and destroyed all my things. Well, not broken in, exactly. The door was unlocked and not actually damaged. I'm sure it was Rob. I overheard something you need to know about. Call me back. I assume I shouldn't touch anything? Or should I drive back to Penzance?' She went outside, gulping in the fresh air. Somehow, the entire cottage felt polluted, the peace destroyed and suddenly it seemed to be living up the locals' saying, Bodilly Cove. It's a bad place. It certainly felt that way at that moment.

Emma kept looking at her phone, wondering why Sam didn't call back. Should she call the police station? There was some special number you were supposed to call but she couldn't remember what it was. She dialled 999 and asked for the police. As clearly as she could, she described the problem.

'And are you or is any one else injured?'

asked the police woman, presumably in a call centre somewhere.

'No, I'm fine but very shaken.'

'Do you have someone you can call to be with you?'

'Not really. I'm sort of on holiday here. The Penzance station knows about the situation. It's a long story.'

'Penzance is the nearest town, I gather.'

'Yes.'

'Leave it with me, then. I'll get someone to you as soon as possible,' the woman said reassuringly.

'Should I just leave everything as it is?'

'Probably best. Try not to worry. Help is on the way.'

'Thanks,' Emma mumbled and switched off the phone.

How long would it take for anyone to get here? She thought of going back to the comforting kitchen of Mrs Crelly but somehow, she felt she couldn't trust anyone any more.

Rob couldn't have wasted any time in getting here. She had sat by the hedge outside his cottage for possibly half an hour. He could scarcely have left when she arrived back.

Emma shuddered. Suppose she had come in when he was using his knife. She now knew he had killed at least once, so perhaps he would have finished her off without a thought. He'd have tossed her over the cliff no doubt, or stuffed her into the car and set it alight.

She began to shake at the thought and felt very sick, wrapping her arms round herself in an attempt to stop shaking. *Pull yourself together,* she thought hysterically, *what on earth should I do now?*

Her few belongings were no longer usable; she didn't even have a clean pair of pants left. Her toothbrush . . . well, even if it was still there, she didn't fancy using it again. Who could tell what had happened to it?

After what seemed like hours, Emma heard someone approaching. She stood up slowly, hoping it wasn't Rob and his friend and praying it might be Sam. When she saw that it was the detective she had seen previously and another colleague, she almost collapsed with the relief.

'Miss Peterson. Hello. You remember me? Eva Thompson. This is my colleague, DC Fran Harper.'

'Hi. Thank you for coming.'

'So, do you want to tell us what happened?'

'Come inside and look for yourselves.'

Emma showed them in to the kitchen and they looked at the shambles inside.

'Heavens. Someone really went to town. Vandalism, sheer vandalism. Have you any idea who might have done this?'

'Oh yes. I'm pretty certain it was Rob Grenville. I overheard him talking to someone, you see. He was ordered to get rid of me using whatever means it took. This is a threat. Upstairs, he put the report of the burnt car on top of my bed. If that wasn't supposed to scare me into leaving, I don't know what is.'

As she finished the sentence her voice crumbled and she found herself crying as if she would never stop. All the pent up anguish of the past few days rose up and she felt as if she was falling into a deep pit.

The two officers caught her just as she began to sway. 'Come outside again,' Eva Thomson said gently. 'You've been under great stress and this was all just too much for you.'

They led Emma to the bench outside and she sat down.

DC Harper went back inside and began making notes while the sergeant sat beside Emma and asked her to describe everything that had happened since her last visit to the station.

Uppermost in Emma's mind was the conversation she had overheard outside Rob's cottage. She tried to explain it all but kept breaking down when she mentioned Charlie.

'I can see it would be very upsetting, and you're quite right. This vandalism is almost certainly designed to make you go away and leave this place. If what you think you heard is correct, it certainly does sound as if they've got Charlie hidden away somewhere. I'm just not sure why they would keep her a prisoner all this time.'

'It all sounds so farfetched, doesn't it? I mean, what are they actually doing? What's the point of all this?'

'We've had our suspicions that there's a ring operating to bring illegal immigrants into the country. Some people are so desperate they pay all their life savings to get here. Lord knows why. This country has difficulties of its own. But there are people all over wanting to get them here. They put them into terrible conditions and pay them next to nothing just to get the work done. It costs too much to employ British labourers to pick fruit, daffodils, vegetables or do the fish processing. These poor souls are willing to put up with terrible conditions, expecting they can eventually find homes here and even bring their families over. But when each season is over, they're turned out.'

'It all sounds so unlikely. Like some TV drama.'

'I know. We haven't been able to pin point anywhere as a centre yet. I have colleagues working on it but I think this may be one of the beaches where they're landed. This cottage and others along the coast are probably being used as stop off points. It's remote, no road access. It's perfect. Historically, this sort of place is where the smugglers worked. Wreckers too, I shouldn't wonder.'

'And when Martha died, they planned to go

159

on with it. They obviously didn't know Martha had any relatives and assumed the place would just be there to be used by someone else.'

'Possibly. You suggested that Rob was actually responsible for Martha's death?'

'It certainly sounded like it. I assume Rob was angry and lost his temper with her. I'm guessing but he probably hit her with something and then arranged it to look as if she fell.'

'I haven't read the case notes but I thought it was a verdict of accidental death.'

'So I understand. They could have got it wrong, though. Maybe they then stripped the cottage of the decent furniture and sold it on for the money.'

'That's possible. We'll ask around.'

'But this doesn't help with finding Charlie. The man I didn't recognise said they'd have to take her on a boat trip. I guess that was the code for disposing of her?'

Tears filled Emma's eyes again as she voiced her fears.

'Possibly. But it's no use thinking like that. Remember, we're not on hundred percent certain it wasn't her in the car.'

'Oh, I missed something out!' Emma suddenly remembered. 'One of the people they were smuggling in had died on the way and it was her they put in the car. At least, that's what it sounded like.'

She repeated the words as best as she could

remember them. 'He was angry that the man bringing them had actually landed her.'

'We're going to have to go back to the station to make a proper formal statement. Then we need to find you somewhere to stay. You obviously can't come back here. It's too dangerous.'

'But you'll arrest Rob Grenville, won't you?'

'We don't have actual proof. It could be a story you made up, if you think about it.'

'Don't be ridiculous!' snapped Emma. 'How could I make up all of that?'

'I'm not saying that you did, not at all, but it would be your word against his, so we have to find evidence. I'll make the case for a search warrant for his whole place and we'll get a team over there as soon as possible.'

'If they're as desperate as you seem to think, why not just get rid of Charlie right away? Why keep her somewhere?'

'I simply don't know. Now, we need to get you away from here. Is there anything you need to bring with you?'

'Just my shoulder bag. I never want to see the rest of my things ever again.'

'So you'll need to buy some new stuff? We'll go back to the station and then I'll get someone to go shopping with you.'

'Thank heavens for credit cards.'

'You should be able to claim some of it back on insurance. I'll see if DC Harper has finished inside.'

The two officers took a few minutes before they came back outside again.

'I heard a lot of what you said,' the constable said. 'I was taking a look round the kitchen. There's a large spanner at the side of the cooker. Must be used for connecting the gas bottles. I haven't touched it but I think it may have been used to inflict the blow to Martha's head—if there was a blow used to kill her, that is. Have you got an evidence bag?' she asked.

Eva dipped into her shoulder bag and produced a large plastic bag. Using latex gloves, she put the heavy object into the bag and sealed it.

'We'll get forensics to look at it. Even after so long, there may be evidence of blood and possibly hair on it. We'd better lock up now and leave everything as it is. We'll get SOCO to come down. The walk will do them good. How have you been managing? I didn't see your car parked at the top.'

'I've been driving over the farm field. I've got a hire car. It's parked behind the hedge here. I can drive you back to your car if you like, to save you the walk.'

'Thank you. Do you have the key to lock up?'

'Well yes, but is there any point? Whoever got inside has got their own key anyway.'

'Good point. Look, you'd better stay here Fran. I'll ask the team to come back right away. You can get a lift back with them. I'll go back with Emma here and get her sorted for the night.' Eva turned back to Emma and added, 'Leave Fran your key anyway, would you?'

They went through the fence and drove back to the car park where the unmarked police car was waiting. Eva called the police station to get the scene of crime officers organised.

'If you follow me into the town, you can park in our car park,' she told Emma.

As they drove in convoy again back to Penzance, Emma's fears had turned once more into anger. If she'd had Rob in front of her she'd have been ready to cut him into little pieces to get the truth out of him. He may not be very bright but he was most definitely evil. She couldn't even see his desire for the money he earned from all of this, since he lived in near squalor from what she could make out and evidently drove a battered old car. Why did he want money?

There was a parking space at the back of the station. They went inside through a rear entrance and avoided the main desk. 'Is Sam still here?' Emma asked.

'I'll see. Have a seat for a minute and I'll check,' Eva replied before she went through a series of doors and came back a few minutes later. 'He's not back yet. I'm not sure where he is but it's not here. Sorry.'

'Does he know why I'm here?'

'I don't think he does. I'm not sure where he is at present.'

'His mother knew Martha and I think because of that, she invited me to stay with them. I'm sure she would still be willing to give me a bed.'

'That would be good. We'd know you were safe, then.'

'Not exactly the sort of holiday I was planning. This time last week, I was happily planning what to bring down with me. So much for coming to peaceful Cornwall.' She was getting over her earlier anguish.

Eva collected sheets of paper and a pen and sat down.

'I've asked for some tea to be brought. Don't know about you but I'm gasping. I'll try not to take too long. We need to get you some basic things. Toothbrush, toiletries and so on. Will one of the supermarkets do?'

'There's a big one I went to before. They even sell things like undies. I've got nothing other than I'm wearing at this moment.'

'OK, we'll get that organised later, but for now, if you would be so kind, we have a statement to prepare.'

They sat opposite each other and DS Thompson wrote down as she spoke. Emma signed it in the end and they both leaned back again.

'Thank you,' Emma said softly. 'It's been

pretty traumatic. I'll go shopping next and then go and to stay with Sam's mother. I still can't get over what's been done to the cottage. It's all like a dream. One I'd rather forget.'

'I'm sure you would. You'll have to move everything in the end but not until you feel ready to do it. Thank you very much. I'll give Mrs Henley a call for you. Then you can go over whenever you're ready.'

'Thank you for that too. I hope you get these awful people. They have a lot to answer for.'

Emma left the officer and went out to the reception area. Sam was still not back and she hesitated, waiting for someone to tell her what to do. She needed to go shopping and wondered if she should just go.

'Excuse me,' she said to the officer at the desk. 'I need some shopping but I'm not really sure if I should just go.'

'Hang on. I'll make some enquiries.' He went through to the back and returned moments later. 'I thought you shouldn't just go on your own like that. One of our officers will accompany you. If you take a seat over there, someone will come through when they're ready.'

'Well, thank you. Sam still isn't here yet? Only I was hoping to see him before I leave.'

'I'm afraid not. He won't be in 'till much later. Do you want me to give him a message?'

'It's OK, thanks anyway.'

Emma went to sit at the side and waited. It was getting late and she was afraid the supermarket would be closing. After a while she went to the desk again.

'Look, it's alright. I'll go on my own. It's not important that someone comes with me. I feel OK again now.'

'Are you sure? It won't take them long.'

'I'll go now. Thanks anyway.'

She went outside and found the way to her car. She was just about to leave when Sam came back.

'Hello,' he said in surprise. 'What are you doing here?'

'Oh Sam, I can't begin to say! They've broken into my cottage and cut up all of my things. Put coffee and milk powder over everything. It's a total shambles . . .'

'Oh Emma, I am so sorry! That's settled it, you're certainly moving to our place. I insist.'

'It's all been fixed. I am going to your mother's place after I've been shopping.'

'I'm so glad you're moving out now, quite relieved in fact. I'm on duty 'till late so you'll have to go along by yourself. Is that OK?' Sam looked anxious.

'I'll be fine. I need to go and buy a few things but I suspect it won't take me long. I've abandoned finding anything worth keeping.' She shivered. 'Not that I'd want to anyway.'

'I'm off tomorrow, so just get what you need for tonight and we can go shopping properly together tomorrow, alright?'

'That sounds wonderful. I'll look forward to it. But I'm not giving up. I should warn you, I intend to go on looking for Charlie. I'll see you later on.'

Emma left him standing there, watching her go off on her own. She felt angry and sad all at once but she was determined to follow through her plans. Whatever happened next, she was very firm in her ideas.

Thank goodness she still had Charlie's scarf in her bag. That little treasure was still her own.

# CHAPTER 11

It was past eleven o'clock. Sam had returned home and the two of them sat chatting, planning their next move, but Emma didn't want to listen to him when he suggested that she should leave it to the police now.

'I can't do that, Sam,' she repeated for the umpteenth time. 'I have to go and look for Charlie. It's what they all want and I'm not going to leave it.'

'Then I'll have to come with you, won't I? So where do you want to start?'

'I don't really know. I'm assuming that Charlie isn't at Rob's house but he does know where she is. I'm wondering if she might be at the place where the woman are living, the ones who work at the fish place. What do you think?'

He frowned and gave a shrug. 'You could well be right. OK, so we need to find out where that is.'

'I suspect it's not far outside Penzance. They come in by bus each day, don't they? Mini bus, that is. The girl who works in the shop told me that much.'

'We'll go there in the morning. Ask again which direction it comes from. We might even see it and follow it back. How does that sound? But for now, I'm bushed. I really need to go to bed.'

'OK. You make the choices. I just tell you what to choose.' She gave him a cheeky smile.

'Do you need anything else?' he smiled back.

'No thanks. Your Mum has fed me and given me everything I needed. I bought a nightie and some toiletries so I'm all set. Thanks, Sam. Thank you for everything.'

'Don't mention it. Now, let's get to bed. It's going to be a long day tomorrow.'

They went upstairs and settled down for the night, but Emma lay awake for some time, her mind running round all the different ideas she had thought of.

Where was Charlie? What had happened to her? Emma hoped that she was going to get to wherever they were keeping her before they decided to get rid of her. At last, Emma eventually fell into a deep sleep and didn't awake until eight o'clock and when she went downstairs, it was to find Sam had already gone out.

'I don't understand. Why did he go without me?' she asked his mother.

'I think he had some idea or another and he went off, see, wanted to look into it. Don't you worry about him, dearie. Now, what would you like for breakfast?'

'I don't really want too much, thank you. You filled me up last night. Just some coffee and toast maybe?'

'You sure dear?'

Emma nodded and Joan went to make it.

'It won't be long. I've put the coffee pot on so we can share some nice coffee later. Now, what are you going to do today?'

'Well, I'm not sure now. I was planning to go out with Sam this morning. Do you know where he's gone?'

'Afraid not, dear. He was anxious to go on his own. I expect he'll be back again before too long.'

They sat together drinking coffee. Emma was impatient to be going out and kept looking through the window but Sam didn't come back.

'I think I may go off on my own, too,' she said finally. 'I really do have to visit the place where I think Charlie might be being held. I need to go to the village along the coast and see what I can find out.'

'Well just you take care, dear. It's important you don't get yourself into trouble, you know.'

'I won't. I was going to wait for Sam but tell him I've gone on ahead, will you?'

She went back upstairs and got herself ready to go. It was just a matter of collecting her things together. She went down again and got into her car and was halfway along the lane when she saw Sam coming back.

'Where have you been?' she demanded anxiously.

'Come back to the house and I'll tell you.'

He started off again and in exasperation, she turned the car in the narrow lane and followed him back to his house.

'I went to the fish place and asked someone to tell me where the women came from. Nobody knew. They only come on Mondays and Thursdays. The other days, they go and work somewhere else.'

'Oh. So where do they go?'

'They go to a farm somewhere out on the road towards Lands End. Are you up for visiting there?'

'Yes indeed. Let's go.'

'Hang on a minute. We need to think about it and get organised. I can go in my uniform but you're not authorised to wear anything official. I think I should go alone.'

'No, no no, I want to come with you. I

needn't say very much. Just keep writing things down and looking round everywhere, look like I'm official or something.'

'I won't wear uniform then. I'll go in my civvies and we can see what we can find.'

'OK. I think it's for the best.'

'Am I allowed a cup of coffee, before we go then?'

'If you must, but don't take forever drinking it,' she said with a laugh. She was feeling tense but didn't want him to see it.

*       *       *

They set off in Sam's car and were soon driving west, past Penzance, then continued along the road towards the end of the county and began to feel as if they were not going anywhere.

'I think we might need to go off this road, you know. I suspect they live somewhere hidden away,' Sam said.

'You're right. I think this leads us nowhere fast. Let's stop and look at the map.'

They poured over it and saw endless roads off to either right or left. They decided to explore them and set off looking hard at every turning. It was a totally wasted effort. Each time they went along a track, it turned into a yard and they had to turn back onto the road.

'This is all pointless,' Emma said at last.

'I agree. There aren't many side roads left that we haven't investigated and it's almost one o'clock. Why don't we take a break and go and find a pub for a sandwich?' Sam suggested.

It had proved to be a useless day so far and they were almost ready to give up. They sat quietly eating sandwiches, listening to everyone who came into the pub. A couple of blokes came in and both sat in the corner with pints of bitter. They were busily conversing and hadn't noticed Sam and Emma.

'We need to move the girl. You know what I mean?'

'Yer, well I can see as how you need the space. She's about done it for us, 'asn't she?'

'We need to get rid of her. Can I leave it to you?'

'Course. I'll call in there on my way back.'

'She 'asn't signed that paper yet, mind you. I'll 'ave one more go at making her do it then I'll have to let 'er go. I don't like it but I'll have to forge her signature.'

'Right. You're the boss.'

Sam was totally silent and urged Emma to remain quiet too.

'It's Rob. I know it's him,' Emma whispered urgently. 'I'm keeping my head down in case he sees me and recognises me.'

'He doesn't know me so you stay low. I'll go and pay and we can get outside into the car when they move.'

Sam went over to the bar and chatted easily to the bartender for a while before he came back and sat down again. At last, the two men got up and went to the bar, dumped their glasses and strode off.

Emma and Sam followed as quickly as they could and she looked away so she wasn't seen. The two men got into their cars and each of them drove off in the opposite direction.

'Now where do I go?' asked Sam.

'Follow the other guy. I don't know where he's going but it would seem a good idea.'

They drove after him, keeping a short distance away. He suddenly turned off the main road and went down a narrow lane, leading eventually to a farm house. Sam was behind him, a good few yards back.

'Now what? I can't follow him into his own yard.'

'Suppose I was to walk in there and ask for a drink?'

'Don't be ridiculous. I'm not letting you do that.'

'We have to do something. I can't be this close to Charlie and just leave her there. I just can't do it, Sam.'

'I don't know. Damnation, I can't let you go alone. We'll both go together. Curse you, Emma!'

'OK, let's both go. We'll think of something to say when we get there.'

They parked their car to one side of the building, both looking round as if to see where the shelter was. It looked somewhat sterile to both of them. They looked everywhere but could not see where so many people could possibly be living. It all seemed to be well ordered and looked good.

'It's no use. There really isn't anywhere they could be staying. We need to move on and think about it some more.' Sam was beginning to feel they were wasting time.

'I can't help thinking there is something we're missing here though,' Emma said anxiously.

They went back to their car and drove away, but Emma kept looking back as they went down the farm track and didn't see anyone at all.

'We got away with that little episode. Nobody saw us at all.'

'I don't know. I feel as if someone was watching us all the time. We just didn't get challenged. It was very strange.'

'It's your conscience that does it. Makes you feel guilty when you're not,' Sam said. 'So, what now? We still don't know who that was. We don't have any idea about who is responsible for what. I think we should just go home and let the detectives deal with it, Emma.'

'I can't Sam. I can't just give up.'

'So, where do you want to go now?'

'I don't know.'

'We're heading back near to Penzance.' He stopped the car in a layby and they sat for a few minutes, trying to take stock of what they knew already and the people they knew who might be involved in whatever this was.

'There are the people at the garage,' Emma said. 'Harry in the workshop and Lucinda in the shop. There's the ghastly Colin. He's much older than I was expecting. Then there are the Crellys, but they all seem quite innocent in all of this. That chap we followed. Do we know who he is?'

'No, but I expect someone else will tell me if I asked.'

'Rob we know, of course. Is that the whole list?'

'Looks like it. Not very much to go on, is it?'

'I suspect there are more people around. People who know about some of this. I really suspect that Lucinda knows more than she's letting on. She looked shocked when I mentioned some of the furniture. Should we go and see her again?'

'We could do. I'm not too keen though. I don't know what to ask her, or how to do it,' Sam objected.

'Let's get back to your mum. At least she's not going to ask us questions we can't answer.'

They drove back and told Joan of their fruitless search. 'Come on and sit down. I'll make a pot of tea and you can tell me what you've heard,' she told them.

'Thanks. We need to go out again later, though. I don't want to sit and waste time. I'm not really sure where we're going but it feels as if we must go somewhere.'

'I'm not too happy just driving round aimlessly,' Sam told Emma. 'I mean to say, if we have something in mind then I'm happy to follow it, but . . .'

'I don't want you to drive aimlessly, Sam, but I feel as if something is about to happen and I want to be there when it does. I can go off again on my own. I don't need you to come with me, you know.'

Emma felt near to tears but wasn't going to show it.

'Come on now,' Sam said softly. 'I'm not giving up on you. I just don't want you to be so blind. You have to see that it's pointless just going from one place to the next with nothing positive, nothing organised.'

'I am not giving up,' Emma said, her chin tilted defiantly.

'I'm not asking you to. Just let's be practical and decide where you want to go to and why and I'll happily drive you.'

'Oh, I just don't know, I really have no idea.' Emma was starting to get upset again and feeling frustrated. 'I want to go back to see Lucinda. She knows something but I'm not sure what. And Harry too. Let me go into the shop to buy something, anything. I can try to get her to tell me what she's hiding. I can do that on my own.' She had made up her mind.

'Well, OK then, you go ahead and do that and I'll wait here. But if you're not back soon,

I'll come after you.'

*　　　*　　　*

Feeling better, Emma drove up to the garage, went into the shop and picked up a paper. That would do for now. There was someone else at the counter and she waited.

'Hello love. How are you getting on?'

'I'm OK, thank you. I gather you know what's happened to me? Everything at the cottage has been vandalised, so I'm not staying there any more.'

'I did hear. I'm so sorry dear. So, where are you staying?'

'I've got a B&B organised in the next village.'

'That's nice.'

'Yes. I was wondering . . .' Emma began. 'When I mentioned that Martha's furniture had all been moved, you looked a bit . . . well, startled. Can I ask why?'

'Oh, no reason, dear. I was just a bit surprised, that's all. Now, can I get you anything else?'

'Was there a reason why you were surprised?'

'Of course not, dear. Now, if there's nothing else?'

She clearly wanted to be rid of her customer.

'No, nothing else, thank you.'

That was all a pointless bit of nonsense, she thought, annoyed. She would go into the garage next and ask Harry a few questions.

'Oh hello dear,' he said as she went inside. 'You finished with the car then?'

'No, not at all. I just wanted to make sure it's OK for me to keep it a little longer?'

'It's perfectly alright. Are you planning on staying around here then? Only I heard as you'd left your cottage.'

'Well, yes, I have. I was going to tell you. I'm staying in the next village along from here, in a B&B. I don't expect to be there for long though.'

'I'd better have a note of it, then. You've still got the same phone number, haven't you?'

'Yes, that's the same.' She gave him the address only she changed the number of the Henley's cottage to another one. She would let him know later when he was cleared of suspicion, if it was only in her mind.

'So, have you heard any more about the furniture that was taken?' she asked him.

Harry looked puzzled. 'No. I don't know about no furniture. Haven't heard about that. I knew there wasn't much at the cottage and you were sort of managing.'

'I was managing, it was left without anything much, and I bought a few bits and pieces to see me through. But the whole lot was trashed. Have you heard anything about that?'

'Oh, dear me, no. It sounds as if you got a

right going over.'

'Yes. It's all been a bit traumatic. Lucky I found somewhere to stay, wasn't it?'

'Very lucky indeed. Oh dear me.' He did seem very concerned about her, she thought.

'Well, I'd best be getting back now,' she told him. 'Thanks for being so sympathetic.'

'I'm so sorry dear. Not a good feeling about Cornwall, is it?'

'Not at all. It's all made me very doubtful about staying here but I will for another day or two.'

'Weel, goodbye then, dear. You'll let me know about the car, won't you?'

'I will. And thanks again.'

*     *     *

Emma drove back to the Henleys, where she mentioned everything she had picked up on at the garage.

'So, as you can see, I'm not too happy that Lucinda was a bit doubtful but I did feel happier that Harry was sympathetic.'

'I suppose that says something.'

Sam was dubious about the whole exercise and it showed.

'I suspect that Lucinda is sitting on her chairs she bought from Rob and is feeling guilty now. I suppose it's just a gut feeling I have and I've no way of proving it. I might see if I can find out where she lives and go round to take a look.'

'You mustn't go, Emma. This is a lot more important than you think. Don't be stupid. You hear me?'

'Yes, but I'm just feeling frustrated. There has to be something we can do.'

'We'll sit for a few minutes and decided exactly what we need to do next. Who we need to talk to. Who is suspicious. OK?'

'Yes, boss.'

Emma was aware that he was only trying to protect her and keep her out of danger, but she couldn't help feeling frustrated and that things were just not moving along as quickly as they could do. She *had* to find Charlie before anything dreadful happened to her.

Only seconds later, she spoke again.

'Actually, we should go to Rob's cottage and see if he can shed some light on all of this. He must be guilty of doing all that damage to Martha's cottage, surely.'

'If he's there. I suspect he may have been arrested by now.'

'But we saw him this morning.'

'Yes, but he was on his way back here. At least, we think he was,' Sam replied.

'He seems to have been coming back. Suppose he went off somewhere else? Suppose he went to see Charlie?'

Immediately, they drove off to Rob's cottage, parking in the car park at the top of the lane. It seemed quiet and deserted, no sign of Rob or of his car.

'I don't like it. It's too quiet here,' Emma said.

'Like I said, he's probably been taken into custody. I thought that would happen yesterday, actually.'

'But suppose he's gone to Charlie? He might have . . . oh good lord, he might even be stabbing her right now! We've got to go and find her. She clearly isn't here.'

'Maybe she did send that text to you. Perhaps she is competent after all.'

'Maybe, but I don't think she did send it, not for a minute, not Charlie. At least she didn't send it willingly.'

'OK, it was just a suggestion.'

'Who do you think that chap was we followed this morning?'

'I don't know. One of the many hundred who live out there.

Why? You're not thinking of going back there are you?'

'No, but he must have some connection with it all. He was talking to Rob wasn't he?'

'I think you're grasping at straws. Look, I'll give them a call at the police station. I'm on duty again tomorrow but it might ease your mind. Come on, let's get back to the car. This place is much too quiet and I don't like it at all.

# CHAPTER 12

Rob Grenville had disappeared. The police had been to his cottage the previous evening and found nobody there. The place was deserted and they had got inside and looked around but had discovered nothing. They had been back today but still nobody was there. Sam was told this when he called and he repeated it to Emma.

'Come on. Let's get away from here. I don't like it here and I don't think he's going to show again.'

'So, what do you think has happened to him?'

'I don't really know. I'm quite at a loss over all of this.'

They went back in silence, both were thinking and had little to say. When they arrived at Sam's home, his mother had prepared them a meal, though neither of them felt much like eating, they sat politely and made a fair attempt.

'You're a pair of miseries,' Joan said after a while. 'Come on, cheer up. It's not as if you're both suffering a major loss.'

'Sorry Joan, but I do feel as if I've suffered a loss. Though I didn't like Rob, I feel as if something has gone out of our lives.'

'I'm sorry dear. I didn't know. Have you

heard something you're not mentioning?'

'No, not really. I'm just very afraid that something dreadful has happened to Charlie. It was hearing them talking this lunch time. I've been feeling very bad ever since.'

'Come on now. We'll have one last trip out this evening,' Sam said. 'Have one last look around for her. Not that I have any idea where we should start.'

'Can I help with the dishes?' she asked.

'Not at all. You go and do whatever you need to do.'

'Thank you. It was a lovely meal.' But Emma was just being polite—she actually had no idea what she'd eaten.

They drove to Rob's place again, to see if he had turned up but it remained as they had left it. They were both concerned about him.

'We could try Colin's place. See if he's there.'

'Let's give it a go.'

Sam drove to Langton and they quickly found the row of cottages, where they knocked on the door but it, too, was deserted. They looked at each other but said nothing. It was becoming all too common a series of events.

'What now?'

'I'm at a loss what to suggest, now. I suppose we have to give up and go back home,' Emma said despondently.

'I guess so. Sorry.'

They drove to the turning but suddenly,

Sam drove on, passing it by, went on towards Penzance and then drove on through it.

'Where are we going?' Emma asked.

'Out to that place where we went this afternoon.'

'What are we going to do there?'

'See if the other people are there. There must be something going on there. It must be where they keep their workers. We know they're not at Rob's place nor are they at Colin's. They must have somewhere else to keep them.'

'We shall see then. I hope you're feeling strong enough to cope with them.'

'Course I am. See the muscles?' He held his arm up to show off his biceps and laughed. But it was a nervous laugh and Emma wasn't at all convinced.

They arrived at the place and drove up quietly. Sam parked behind the largest barn and they went around it to the front.

'We've looked all round here. What are you expecting to see?' Emma whispered, not wanting to be heard.

'I thought we might take a look at the house itself. There must be a lot of rooms inside. Keep quiet now. We don't want to be heard.'

They went to the side of the house and peered in through several windows but could see nothing at all. It was reaching ten o'clock and was almost dark. Sam beckoned Emma round the next corner, this time at the rear of the house. The windows were all blackened out.

She made signals to him to be cautious and they crept on round, wondering if and when they were going to be stopped, but everywhere remained quiet.

'It's no good,' she whispered at last. 'I can't see anything, can you?'

'Not at all, no. Come on. Let's get out of here.'

They walked back towards the car when suddenly, a man stepped out in front of them.

'What you doin' 'ere?'

'We're lost and looking for someone to help us. Can you please tell us where—'

Sam suddenly broke off as he was hit on the side of the head from behind.

'Sam!' Emma yelled. 'Sam!'

'Come with me, you.'

Emma's arm was caught and held firmly as she was dragged to an underground cellar. The man opened the cover and gave her a hearty shove and she fell, stumbling into the depths.

'Hello?' she called. 'Hey, you!'

'Emma?' said a small voice. 'Is that you?'

'Charlie? Charlie! Charlie, is it you?'

'I can't move very far.'

Charlie burst into tears and Emma ran over to her.

'Oh Charlie! Are you alright? You must have been here for ages, absolutely ages.'

'I don't feel too good. I'm scared out of

185

my wits.'

'What have they threatened?

'They keep saying things like they'll k-kill me.' She was silent for a moment. 'But what are you doing here?'

'I'm afraid I got caught. Oh dear, what a mess. Sam's been hit on the head and I don't know what's happened to him.'

'Who's Sam?'

Emma went back to the door and gave it a massive shove but it didn't move. She stamped on the floor and bashed the door with her fist.

'Damn! I hope he's OK. They hit him hard with something.'

'Who is Sam,' Charlie repeated.

'Sorry, love,' Emma said, turning back to her friend. 'Sam's a policeman. He was helping me to look for you. Oh lord, what have they done to him?'

'Come here, Emma. Sit down on the bed with me and tell me what you can.'

'I'm sorry. You tell me your part of the story. I can't believe you've been here all this time.'

'I haven't. I was kept at Rob's place for a while. He locked me inside one of his rooms. Then they brought me here. It's only been two or three days . . . I think . . . oh, I don't know. I'm sort of muddled. It may have been longer.'

There was a noise outside the room and they both fell silent, clutching each other. The door was opened again.

'Come 'ere you.'

'She can't move. You've chained her to the bed.'

'Yer, that's right.' It was Colin. 'I meant you.'

Emma recognised his voice. Slowly she rose and crossed the room, wondering if she could make some sort of dash.

'Don't think of trying anything,' he said and she stopped. 'I said come 'ere, 'ands out in front.'

She stuck her hands forward, still not knowing what was about to happen next. It was brighter outside the room and she was briefly dazzled.

Colin reached for her and clipped on handcuffs, then whipped her across to one side if the door and fastened her to a chain as well.

'There. That sorts you out too. Now you can't sit all cosy together, plotting things.'

He slammed the door and she heard him locking it.

'That's done for me,' she whispered to herself. She heard Charlie sobbing and she called out to her. 'It's OK, Charlie, I'm still here.'

'However will we get out of this?'

'God knows.' They both fell silent for a while.

'Oh Charlie. I'm so worried about Sam but it's so good to see you again. Well, not actually seeing you, but . . .'

187

'It's OK, I know what you mean.'

'I have to find out what happened to Sam.'

'It's my guess that they won't come back here tonight. I don't know what they'll do with him. Don't be surprised if they . . . well, do something dreadful to him . . .'

'What do they want you to do? Why are you still here?'

'They want me to sign away my rights to the cottage, but I've refused. It may not be up to much but it is mine and I want it to stay mine.'

'I don't blame you, but, you need to be careful. I think they're about to sign themselves, forge your signature or something. Then I don't know what will happen to you.'

'Now you're here, too, they'll have to do something.'

'That's what's so worrying.' Emma gave a shiver.

'I think we need to be rested when they come back tomorrow. Ready to bash them or something.'

'What have you got to bash them with?' Emma called out.

'Nothing at all. Sorry.'

'I can't move now. I'm stuck over here.'

'That's just great. You haven't even got anywhere to sit.'

'Don't worry about me.'

Whatever she had said about them needing to sleep, Charlie was much too anxious and she kept asking Emma questions. When she heard about the mess the cottage was in she cursed them out loud.

'So, tell me about what happened to you?' Emma said.

'I arrived at the cottage and saw the state it was in. It was a lovely spot but I knew I was going to need to do a load of work on making it habitable, so I went to the shop to buy stuff and I saw the cards, so I sent one. I still desperately wanted you to come, you see.'

'Yes, I did notice that.'

'Then I went back down to the cottage and left the milk and stuff in the kitchen, then decided to walk down to the beach.' There was a moment's silence, before she added with a sigh, 'Oh, don't get at me.'

'I never said a word. So this was all on the Saturday afternoon, was it?'

'Well yes. I was thinking that I needed to get the place cleaned and sorted.'

'Were you expecting it to be empty of furniture?'

'No, not really. I sort of thought I'd manage. I could go and eat out somewhere and start the big clean up the next day. I went down to the beach and into that huge cave. That's when trouble hit me.'

'What happened?'

'Rob happened, that's what. I discovered his name later. He sort of fell upon me and that's when I dropped my scarf. On purpose, of course. I thought if it was there, someone would come after me.'

'I did find it. I took it to the police station. I've still got it . . .' Realisation hit Emma. 'Oh, heavens. I haven't. It's still in my bag in the car. God, I wonder how Sam is? They really hurt him.'

'You seem keen on him.'

'On Sam? Not really.'

Emma was glad she could hide her blushes in the darkness of the room. She was just beginning to realise that Sam meant a lot to her in what had been only a few days.

'Go on with your story,' she told Charlie.

'Not a lot more to tell you. They kept me locked up at Rob's place. Horrid man. He kept asking me to let him have the cottage. I said no, but he kept on and on. Then I suppose he got sick of me and brought me over to this place. I was feeling quite sick by then. He hadn't been feeding me properly, you see, but I ate it because I wanted to stay compos mentis, you know?'

'Good. So you don't think they are planning to get rid of you?"''

'I don't know. What do you think?'

'I don't know, either.'

'What time is it, do you think?'

'Just after midnight.'

'Sorry. I'll shut up now. We should get some sleep.'

'Oh! what about your phone?' Emma remembered.

'My phone? Oh, yes—they told me to send you a message. I suggested some odd words, so you'd know it wasn't me.'

'It worked fine. I knew you'd never call me hun. But I did try it another time and I got your voice message.'

'Don't know about that one. Maybe he was just putting it on to see how it worked.'

'Maybe. It gave me hope though. That you were still alive . . .'

'Oh Emma. I'm so sorry you got involved in all of this. We really ought to get some sleep.'

Not that they did. They talked for ages, planning what they might do and what might happen to them.

At last, they fell silent and both girls slept until it was almost light. They heard someone coming close and decided that they needed to stay silent. The footsteps moved away.

'What was that?' Emma asked her friend quietly.

'They keep coming to see if I'm awake. I stay quiet for ages and they eventually come in to give me something to eat.'

'I wonder if I'll be given something to eat?'

'Expect so. They have been keeping me fed. Don't want me to pass out, I suppose.'

'You do seem brighter.'

'Oh, I am, but it's you. Having you here with me is brilliant.'

'Not that I can do much chained like this. My wrists are hurting and I can't get

191

comfortable at all.'

'Maybe I should just sign their paper.'

'I doubt they'll let us go that easily. I suspect they're planning something unpleasant. Let's not be complacent about it. Something going to happen and probably very soon.'

'I know. What do you think they'll do?'

'Suppose they say they'll hurt me? What then?'

'They wouldn't dare. Would they?'

'It's not impossible.'

'I don't like this one bit. I'm sorry, I hadn't thought about you being made to suffer.'

'They are very clever these people, Charlie. Believe me, I have no doubts about them, none at all. They've given us the night to spend chatting and I suspect they're about to do something dreadful to one of us.'

The thought quietened them both. It was a sobering time. 'What do you think they'll do?' asked Charlie, her voice trembling. 'It's so difficult. I think if they threaten you, I shall have to sign the cottage away.'

'You can't, love. You mustn't just sign it away.'

'I can. Maybe then they'll let us go. We can go back home again and forget all about this place.'

It was so difficult to know what would happen but Emma felt she knew, only too well.

She took a deep breath and said, 'We've got pretty close to finding what he's got hidden here. Do you know who's here?'

'The women you mean. They're in one of the barns, I think. It's round the other side of the building. They bring them back here every evening and lock them in.'

'Why don't they try to escape?'

'They can't. One of them did make an effort but she was caught and they brought her back. I suspect they beat her, too. They don't speak English.' Charlie paused for a moment.

'So what are we going to do? I have this chain round my ankle so there's not much I can do,' Charlie said despondently.

'And I'm stuck over here.'

'I'm scared, Emma. Really scared. They said I was . . . well, I was as good as dead. I think they meant it.'

'I won't let them, do you hear me?'

Emma was getting fired up again and felt ready to fight.


# CHAPTER 13

Sam woke up with a pain in his head. He felt dizzy and rather sick. He sat up and almost fell back again. It wasn't easy even to remember what had happened the previous evening but things were slowly coming back to him. He tried to sit up again but everything went whirling round, making him want to vomit. He leaned over and did just that. His head was hurting. In fact, most of him hurt.

'You're awake at last, are you?' said a voice.

'Well, I think so,' he snarled sarcastically.

'You know who you are?'

'Sam Henley. A policeman.'

'Very good, son. What were you doing here?'

'I'm really not sure. I came here with . . . with someone. I don't remember who . . .'

'OK. Just you go to sleep again.'

'I don't think I need to go to sleep.' He was having difficulty in making his voice work properly.

'Oh, but you will, very soon. Just you take a sniff of this. There now, it's good isn't it? Breathe deeply, that's it . . . OK lads, he's gone again. Take him to the yard and get rid of him.'

'But shouldn't we keep him for a bit longer? He might have a bit more info.'

'Maybe, but he's a pain. I think we'll put him in his car and set fire to it, like we did the other girl."

'But s'pose they come here? They'll be lookin' for 'im.'

'I guess so. We'll have to get rid of both of them. Charlie too. We've waited long enough, but, let's give it one more go. OK?'

The two men left him sitting in the office. He was the boss and they did as they were told. They went across the yard to the back of the house.

'Shall we try to get the girl to sign again?'

'I reckon we might as well. See if she's a bit more willing now she has her friend there with her.'

'I'll open the door, you watch the other one in case she tries summat,' the other man said menacingly as they approached.

'Get back,' yelled Rob Grenville. 'Don't you try nuthin', understand me?'

'Yes,' Emma said softly. She felt scared, very scared indeed. She took a deep breath and asked after Sam, hoping she sounded a lot braver than she really did.

'What's happened to Sam? What did you do to him?'

'Reckon 'e's a goner. Din't like what we said, did 'e Col?'

'Nah. Din't like it at all.'

'You mean you . . . you finished him off?'

'You could say that.'

Emma felt tears burning her eyes.

'Now shut up you—and you, gerrup.' He pointed from one to the next and Charlie stood. 'Come on then.'

'I can't move more than a few feet. I'm chained, remember?'

'Well, you'll just have to manage where you are, won't you?'

'I don't really think I'm ready to sign anything yet. Not quite in the mood,' she added cheekily.

'You'd better sign it.'

'Yer, you gotta sign it or you'll be done for.'

'I don't have to do anything of the sort,' Charlie said.

'Oh, but you do. If you don't sign it, someone else will do it for you and then it won't matter a damn.'

'One last chance.'

'I don't think so. What do you think Emma? Should I do it or not?' she said, trying to sound brave and flippant.

'I don't think so. I don't think you have to sign anything.' She crossed her fingers, praying that she was saying the right thing.

'Let's leave them. Did you want some breakfast?'

'That sounds good,' Charlie said bravely.

'Well tough luck. You won't be gettin' none.'

Laughing, the two men left the girls. They slumped down again and felt very despondent.

'What happens now?' Charlie asked.

'I don't know. I thought we were probably going to get dragged off somewhere.'

'Doesn't mean we won't be. I don't really believe they've got rid of Sam. Do you?' Charlie asked.

'No. I'm hoping they were just trying to scare us. It's nine-thirty. When do they take the women to work?'

'Earlier than this. I expect they've already

gone.'

'I didn't hear them, did you?' Emma asked.

'Maybe they're still here. They don't take them every day.'

The two girls sat quietly, trying to plan what they were going to do. It was not easy. Charlie was fastened with a chain and padlock and the key had been taken away. It meant she had only a small range available to her.

'I need a pee,' she said.

'Oh. How do you do that?'

'It's pretty basic. An old bucket.'

'I wondered where the smell was coming from. Go on then. Don't mind me.'

Feeling very miserable, they tried to make plans as to what do to do next. Emma began to think that Sam had actually been killed when they hit him. She was angry as well as being scared.

'Do you think what they said was really true? About Sam?'

'I don't know. You never know what to believe.'

They sat for a while longer. Emma was thinking hard but came up with nothing. Charlie sat still, not saying anything much. The first excitement of having her friend nearby was dying fast. She knew what these men were capable of and didn't want to give them any excuse to do anything worse.

'We don't know who is the boss, do we?'

'The chap who owns this whole place, I

197

guess.'

'But who is that? We don't know his name, do we?'

'I did hear someone calling him Harry,' Charlie said.

'Harry? No! It couldn't be him. There's someone called Harry runs the workshop at the garage. Well, I think he does anyway. It must be another Harry, surely.'

'I don't know much about it at all.'

Both were feeling hungry but nobody came with any food. Whatever they had in mind for the two women, nobody came with any plans. They were both wearied but speculating and fell silent, each busy with their own thoughts.

'It's driving me mad, just sitting here. I want to be doing something.' Emma spoke at last. 'I want to hit out at someone. I'm so sick of being stuck here like this.' She was restless.

'I went through all of that. I'm afraid that there's only one end to it all. I may as well sign their nasty bit of paper and let it all go. At least that would draw everything to an end.'

'Maybe, but I don't want my end to be like this. I'm not just giving in. You can if you want to but I don't.'

'I know you're right but what do we do?'

'I really don't know.'

It began again. They went round and round everything they could think of but always came back to the beginning again. They were trapped.

198

'I'm starving. Despite everything, I'm desperate for something to eat. You haven't got anything have you?'

'I told you, no. I ate what they brought me earlier.'

'Ah well. I shall sit here and starve. If they don't give us anything to eat, they'll simply find two poor emaciated bodies.'

'Please don't, Emma. Don't joke about it.'

'Sorry.'

'Having you here makes it all different,' Charlie said.

'Well, we have to keep fighting. Promise me, whatever happens next, you'll stay fighting.'

'I'll try,' said Charlie. 'But I'm so afraid they'll take you away. I won't know what's happening to you.'

'I'll be fine. If they do drag me away, I'll fight them. I promise you, they'll be sorry they ever tried to keep me here.'

'You're so brave. I'll try to be just as brave.'

They were silent again for a long time, each one thinking their worst thoughts. Emma lost any inclination to say anything.

'You still OK, Emma?' Charlie asked at last.

'I'm fine. Well, not really. Sorry.'

\*     \*     \*

It was well into the afternoon before anything happened. The two men, Rob and Colin came into the cellar room.

'Right. You're coming with us now. Leave her there to think of what she should be doin'. Only right, don't you think, Col?'

'Absolutely. Come on. You're comin' with us. You're quite a tasty little piece aren't ya?' Rob said, his hands wandering.

'Stop it,' Emma snapped, but whether she liked it or not, Emma was dragged out.

'Don't worry love. And don't sign that paper, whatever they say,' she called out behind her.

'Shurrup. I tell ya, shurrup.'

'Don't worry about me. I'll be fine.' She was slapped into silence and dragged off.

'Emma! Emma!' Charlie called out.

Emma was dragged over to the main part of the house. She was rebellious all the way and wouldn't go quietly.

'Stop it. Don't try to drag me like that.'

'Shurrup, darn you.'

He slapped her across the face and she did stop making the noise for a moment. She was momentarily shocked as well as feeling terrified. These two were everything she hated most.

'You'll pay for that.' She was furious and didn't want him to think he could get away with it.

'You'll see what you can and can't do. Get in there.'

Emma was shoved into the same room as Sam. He was lying on the floor close to the

200

wall. She ran over to him and went down on her knees beside him.

'Sam! Oh Sam, what have they done to you?'

He was in a deep sleep, induced by whatever drug they had given him, but least he was still alive.

'You can't do this.'

'Oh, but we can, and we can do it to you, too.'

They came over to her and pressed something over her face. She felt herself slipping away and tried hard to resist, but it was no good. Soon, she slumped down unconscious, beside Sam.

'There you go. Now, let's go and get the other one. If she sees what we've done to these two, I reckon she'll agree to do what we tell her. Once we've got her signature for the cottage, we can resume our contracts with Cyan. Go and get her.'

'I'm not sure about this Col. I think she's still got a bit of summat to mek 'er resist us. I doubt we're going to get any results from either of them girls.'

'We'll leave things be and wait 'till Harry comes back.'

# CHAPTER 14

Emma awoke and felt very sick. She lay still while the two men sat smoking and hoped they didn't notice her. She had no idea of what time it was.

'Shall we go and try the other one again?' Colin suggested.

'Nah. Stay 'ere.'

'But if we can get her to sign summat, that's one up to us?'

'You can go and try if you wants. I'm not movin' an inch.'

'Whatever. I might go for a walk around, you know, make sure nobody's come anywhere near.'

'OK.'

Colin got up and stretched, then went to the door, glancing back at the room.

'I s'pose they're still out of it all?' He went over to the pair slumped on the floor and kicked out with his boot. 'Yer. They're still out of it. You comin'?'

'Oh alright. I might as well I s'pose.'

The pair went off and Emma opened her eyes again.

She felt where she'd been kicked and grimaced. It had been so tough not to move at all when it was happening but she felt as if she had succeeded. She rolled over towards Sam.

'Hey, Sam? You awake yet?'

He remained still and though he was breathing, she worried about him. The wound on his head was large and open to anything that was around to infect it. She wondered what to do. If she were to bathe it, assuming there was something she might use, it would alert the men when they returned.

If only she could get out, maybe she could find someone to help her. Slowly, she stood up, still feeling very weird. She went to the window but could see nothing. There was nobody around.

Emma was desperate to get help. She noticed the phone on the wall to one side of the desk. Was it working or just an internal phone? She lifted the receiver and got a dialling tone. She dialled 999 and heard it ringing. All the time, she was looking round her in case the men came back.

'Fire, police or ambulance?' the operator asked her.

'Police,' she whispered urgently. 'Oh, but I need an ambulance, too.'

'I'll give you the police first and you can take it from there.'

'Hello?'

'Where are you?' asked the operator.

'In a farmhouse outside Penzance. Please hurry. I don't know how long I have before someone comes back. We've being held here. I'm a prisoner and I have an injured policeman lying here.'

'Where exactly are you?'

'About three miles—no four miles—from Sennen, towards Penzance.' She rambled on with more details and cursed herself for not being more coherent. 'Please, tell them to hurry. And send an ambulance too. Sam's really hurt.'

Eventually, she had to put the phone down and went back over to Sam.

'Oh Sam, what have they done to you?'

He stirred and she spoke again, quickly. 'Sam, wake up. It's Emma, Sam. Come on, darn you. Wake up Sam.'

But apart from that one little sound he had made, he remained unconscious. She felt so worried about him but she still didn't know what to do.

She sat up and held him, hoping the police would arrive before the two men came back to her. She heard them coming and slumped down again, praying that nobody would notice she wasn't in quite the same position.

They opened the door again and she heard one of them saying, 'It's OK. Still right out of it, the pair of them.'

'Hope you haven't overdone it with that stuff.'

'They'll be alright or they won't.'

He laughed in such a sinister way that Emma felt like getting up and hitting him, but she stayed as still as she could.

The two men went away again, locking the door, but she lay for a moment or two longer. If they could only hold on 'till the police arrived, but it was going to take a while.

After a full five minutes of lying still, Emma rose and went back to the window. There was nothing. She lay down again, expecting the men to come back at any minute.

The next time she looked out, she saw a stranger walking round. She ducked back behind the frame, wondering who it was and then realised it was someone in uniform. A policeman!

Emma hammered on the window but he wasn't hearing her. She went over to the door and shook it. It was firmly locked and there was nothing she could do to open it.

'Hey! Hey you out there!' she yelled but they walked away round to the other side of the building. It was incredibly frustrating and she slumped down in the chair again. After a few seconds she got up again and started hammering at the windows and yelling but the policeman went to the other side.

She gave up and sat down near Sam, who was still deeply unconscious. She stroked his hands and told him to stay with her. Then impatiently she jumped up and began to shout again.

'Somebody, help! Please come here. Please.' She was becoming quite emotional by now and was ready to cry again but she gritted her teeth and shouted again.

Through the window, she could see another car driving down the long drive. It was Eva and Fran. Something had to happen now. She banged on the window again. The two women were out of their car and walking towards the building.

'What was that?' asked Eva. I thought I heard something.'

'I don't know. Where was it coming from?'

'Come on.'

They both ran across the yard and Emma was knocking against the door of the office.

'OK love. Hang on there. We need something to break down the door.'

Emma was so relieved, she felt as if she were about to cry but she stemmed her tears, yelling at them to hurry.

'Come on, please,' she was calling. 'Come on.'

'It's OK. We're just getting something to break the door down. Are you alright?'

'Sort of, but Sam isn't. He needs an ambulance. I'm so worried about him.'

'I'll call one. Here comes Fran with the others. Stand back away from the door.'

There was a couple of loud crashes and the door flew open.

'Oh, thank goodness!' Emma said. 'Look at Sam. He's in a bad way. I woke up ages ago and I tried to wake him but . . .'

She burst into tears.

'It's alright, Emma. You just come away from him. There's not much you can do for him at present.'

'But I can . . .'

'Come away, right away. Go outside and try to get some fresh air inside you.'

'How come you're here? I mean to say, of all the places you could have looked, how did you get so lucky?'

'We were worried when Sam didn't arrive for work this morning. Then his mother phoned to see if we knew what had happened to him. We've been looking pretty well all day. Then you called in and we got the message.'

'I'm glad you didn't give up. Have you found Charlie yet?'

'Charlie? No. Is she here somewhere?'

'She's in the cellar. Oh, Charlie!'

Abandoning everyone, Emma ran across to the side of the house where she knew the cellar must be. She hauled on the doors to pull it open but it too was locked.

'This is ridiculous. I need to get her out. Hang on Charlie!'

'Emma? Is it you? Are you alright?'

'Yes, love. It's me. I can't get you out yet. I need to get them to come over. Hang on, only be a minute.'

Emma went back to the office place and watched in horror as they tried to bring Sam back to consciousness.

'What's going on?'

'It's alright. He isn't dead but he's very sick. If we could have got here sooner, we might have been able to rouse him . . .'

'Oh no! Oh Sam!'

She went down on her hands and knees beside him but he remained in the deepest sleep possible. She bit back her tears.

'Did you find your friend?' asked Eva.

'Yes, but I can't get the door open.' Unwillingly, Emma rose from beside Sam.

'Go on then, Fran, show us what you're made of,' Eva said. 'Go with Emma. Leave us here with Sam. I promise, we'll do all we can to help him.'

Fran and Emma led the way across the yard with the two men carrying the battering ram ready to bash the door down.

'Stand back, right away from the door,' they instructed.

One swing of the battering ram and the door collapsed.

'That didn't take much, did it?' one of the men laughed.

'Emma!' Charlie said in relief as she came out of the cellar and flung her arms round her friend.

'Thank heavens you found me.' She looked at the rest of the group. 'And thanks to all of you, too.'

'You're alright? Aren't you?' Emma asked anxiously. She had quite forgotten her own troubles by now and was just anxious about her friend.

'I'm fine. Glad to be out in daylight again.'

'You're filthy, Charlie, dear. And sorry to say it but you do niff a bit.' Emma found herself laughing and crying at once.

'I doubt you've looked in a mirror lately either.'

'They came and took your chain off?'

'Yes. They were about to drag me off somewhere but then changed their minds.'

'If you two have quite finished,' Fran said to them. 'We need to get you sorted out and you're going to have to spend some time answering questions and helping us catch these people who've been keeping you here.'

They both began to speak at once but them Emma took over. 'It was Rob Grenville and Colin James. They were the main ones. I think Harry was also involved. I don't know his other name but he works at the garage.'

Emma wanted to see all of the men charged and held.

'Were they here with you?' asked Eva.

'Yes, so they must be somewhere around. Aren't they still in the house?'

'They must have scarpered,' said one of the police officers.

'We'd better get out and look for them. I wonder what scared them off?' Charlie said.

'I suspect it was the sight of you lot coming

over,' Emma said. 'Let's get back to be with Sam now we're all safe.'

They trooped across the yard and rejoined those in the office.

'Here comes the ambulance,' Eva said. 'We need to get Sam seen to and you two, you need to get yourselves looked at too. Go to the hospital and get seen by the experts. We'll get Sam's car taken back and you two go in the ambulance.'

'Can I get my bag out of Sam's car first?'

'Alright, but then no more prevarications. Get off to the hospital and get yourselves checked over.'

'I'd like to call Joan, Mrs Henley. Is that alright?'

'We'll do it. I'll make sure she knows all she needs to know. Now, get along with you.'

\*　　　\*　　　\*

The two women were checked over at the hospital and released relatively quickly.

'I am absolutely starving,' Emma announced.

'Then I guess we'd better find some food. I'm pretty hungry too. I expect the canteen's closed by now.'

The two detectives met them at the doorway.

'We were told you were coming out right away. I gather Sam is still there?'

'He's regained consciousness and they're treating his head wound. The good news is that he's going to be alright.' Emma was smiling. 'We're going to get something to eat.'

'I'm afraid you need to come and make preliminary statements,' one of the detectives said.

The two girls looked crestfallen.

'I suppose it can wait until after you've eaten. We've booked you into a hotel for at least tonight.'

'Thank you. We do appreciate you looking after us like this.'

The two girls were fed at the police canteen and afterwards, made their statements. They were totally exhausted and when they had finished, they were taken to the hotel.

'I'm so weary, I could fall asleep where I stand,' Emma said.

\*       \*       \*

The next morning, they had to wear their same dirty clothes, but after a hearty breakfast, they went shopping and bought a new outfit for each of them, using Emma's credit card.

'What a good job I didn't lose it,' Emma told Charlie. 'If I hadn't left it in the car, we'd have been in trouble. Oh, please can you get rid of all that lot?' she asked the shop assistant. 'I never want to see it again.'

'I suppose we'd better get back to the police

station next. See what's been happening,' Charlie suggested.

*    *    *

'You'll be delighted to know that we got them all. They were back at Rob's house deciding what to do next.'

Eva was also feeling very pleased to have cleared up so many of her ongoing cases. 'Really pleased with it all. Thanks to you, we got the whole business sorted.'

'Glad to be of help. We're staying in Penzance for tonight and may go back to Bodilly Cove later today to look at the place and decide what's to be done with it,' Emma said.

'I suspect you'll have your work cut out to make it habitable.'

'We're good at decorating and stuff,' said Charlie.

'First class in fact,' Emma added with a grin.

*    *    *

Two days later, the two girls were at Truro's main hospital, sitting beside Sam who was looking very much better. His head was wrapped in a large bandage and he was sitting up in bed looking as if he wanted to leap out of it at any minute.

'Are you two really alright?' he asked for

212

the fourth time. 'Only I was so worried that you were let out of here too early.'

'For goodness' sake,' they laughed in unison. 'Stop worrying and get yourself better. I've got a bruise or two but that's nothing. I'm not going anywhere 'till I know you're alright again.'

Emma held his hand and squeezed it.

'That sounds good. I was afraid that if I said I was alright again, you'd be off like a shot.'

'They caught the two men and they're after Harry as well. They're all being charged with holding people against their will and with smuggling and robbery. They've been bringing in all sorts of stuff . . . tobacco and alcohol . . . they should be put away for ages,' Charlie told him.

'What happened to the women?'

'They took them off to somewhere else and the police are still trying to discover where they've gone. Evidently, the two men saw them coming back and sent them elsewhere. The man driving them—we assume it was Harry—is missing too.'

'What a mess. So, where are you two staying?' asked Sam.

'In a hotel in Penzance. Only for another day or two. Then we're going to put the cottage into some sort of order, refurnish it and see what happens after that.'

Charlie looked at the other two and suddenly felt as if she was in the way.

'Look, I'm going off to get a cup of something. You don't mind if I leave you two alone for a while?'

'Course not,' said Emma with a smile.

'I wanted to say thank you, Emma,' Sam said softly.

'No need. Really. I didn't do anything much.'

'Well, without you, I'd have been a goner. If you hadn't called for the ambulance when you did, I don't know what would have happened.'

'But I didn't do anything. Really. Now, shut up and settle back. I'm thinking of staying down here, you know. I wanted to give up my job anyway.'

'Really? That is great news. I'm sure you'll find something else very quickly.'

'I'm going to be OK for a while, anyway. I'll help Charlie get the cottage sorted and then we'll see. I only have to give in my notice at the flat and I can move my stuff down here.'

'That's terrific news. Really good. I'm feeling so much better already. I think they'll let me out quite soon.'

'Not too soon. Wait 'till you're absolutely right again.'

'I will, promise. Emma, I wanted to ask you something . . . I don't expect any sort of answer yet but I want you to think about it . . .' he said tentatively.

'What?'

'Would you . . . well . . . would you go out

with me?'

'How do you mean?' Emma said. She didn't mean to sound dim, but she felt a little cagey, not wanting to make assumptions and then feel foolish.

'Well, once I'm over all of this, will you go out with me?' Sam said. 'You know . . . like on dates?'

'Of course I will,' Emma said, smiling. 'But just you make sure you get yourself fully better. I'll leave you to rest up for a bit and go and find Charlie, but we'll come to see you tomorrow.'

# CHAPTER 15

The two girls left the hospital and walked through the town.

'You never actually told me what happened after they took me away from you.'

'Really? You want to hear?' Charlie said.

'Yes,' Emma replied firmly.

'I thought my end was coming. I'm not sure I should say this, but I was pretty near trying to kill myself. I didn't want to go on living. I thought they were coming to finish me off and I didn't want them to succeed.'

'Oh Charlie. For heavens' sake. You must never think like that. You have to fight all the time,' Emma told her friend. 'I had to lie back

215

and take them kicking me and pretend that I was still unconscious, but it worked, and I was able to call the police and then to wave and yell at them when they turned up.'

'I can see that now. I just felt so desperate when they left me on my own.'

'Well, it's all alright now. No more thoughts of killing yourself or anything like it, OK?'

Charlie smiled at her friend.

'Thanks Emma. Thanks for everything.'

'All part of the service. Know what? My car is at Sam's mother's house. We could go and reclaim it. It's a pretty knackered old Fiesta, on hire from Harry himself. We'll have to go and see what's happening to that place now.'

They took a bus to Joan's house and she welcomed them like long lost friends.

'I can't tell you how pleased I was when they told me you were alright. And this must be Charlie. Now, you two girls come and sit yourselves down. I have some fresh scones just out of the oven.'

They looked at each other and laughed.

'There's always something fresh out of the oven here,' Emma said cheerfully. It was a good feeling.

*　　*　　*

They drove back to Penzance and to the hotel, where they got a message from Eva, telling them they had caught the three main men concerned. Harry, Colin and Rob were safely in custody. It was a huge relief to both of them.

'You know something? I feel really concerned about that poor woman who died. It seems terrible that she simply dies on the way here and will be lost forever.'

Emma was thinking about their past few days in Cornwall. 'I'm not sure what we can do about it all,' Charlie said.

'No, nor am I, but we ought to do something.'

\*     \*     \*

They spent the next day or two trying to work out how to bring an ending to it all.

There would be the inevitable trials and sentencing of the men involved in the deals with the smuggling of people but the two girls were more concerned with finishing things for the woman who had died.

'It felt so awful when they told me it was you who had died, Emma told Charlie. 'I didn't want to believe it at all. I just knew it wasn't you and felt nothing but relief. Stupid isn't it?'

'I can understand it perfectly. It must have been terrible for you when you were told that.'

'And now I feel all mixed up about her. It seemed so pointless, to travel all that way and then just die.'

Emma felt tears burning at the backs of her eyes.

'Tell you what,' Charlie suggested. 'Why don't we get in touch with Eva again. She'll know what we need to do.'

Charlie held her friend's hand.

'Thanks, Charlie, that's a good idea.'

*       *       *

It was a week later and the two girls and Sam and one or two others stood at the side of a small grave. The rain was drizzling and seemed to reflect everyone's mood.

The coffin was laid to rest and prayers were said, and it was time to leave.

'It seems a bit sort of all over now, doesn't it?' Sam said.

'All of this part of it all is finished now. We just have to get the cottage put to rights,' Emma said.

'I suppose so. The women have all been sent back to their homes. They have no vast riches to their names, but at least they're alive and back to their normal lives.'

'But we have lives still to be lived,' said Sam. 'And having got so near to ending my life, I'm very glad we have.'

'Come on then. Paint to be bought and brushes and all manner of stuff.' Emma's laughter was a little forced.

'And loads of furniture and bedding and

. . . hey, there's lots of life to be lived.' Sam squeezed Emma's hand reassuringly.

'Goodbye, little lady,' whispered Emma. 'I'm so sorry it all turned out this way.'

She turned and looked at Sam and knew that she had the whole of her future life to live.